I0714355

Also by J.M. Holmes:

Ice, Ice, Baby (*with* Prodigy *and* Time Trial)

They Left Me for Dead

The Fruit-Eating Cat

Energy Spike

A Deep Breath of Water

Waking Up Outside

Little Potato Fries *(collected poems)*

Pro Tem: The Amazing Year *(nonfiction)*

All titles also available in large print and giant print editions

J.M. HOLMES

RETRIEVERS

LITERATI INTERNATIONAL

~ SINCE 1981 ~

Toronto • New York • London

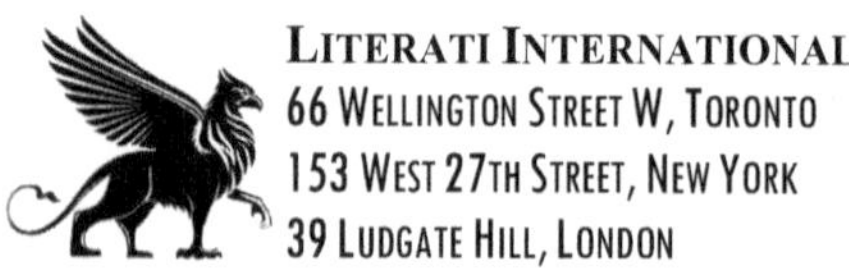
LITERATI INTERNATIONAL
66 WELLINGTON STREET W, TORONTO
153 WEST 27TH STREET, NEW YORK
39 LUDGATE HILL, LONDON

Library of Congress Control Number: 2021909227
ISBN 978-1-7368485-2-4

hic sunt dracones

TABLE OF CONTENTS

the retriever

THE **INSTANT** she opened her eyes Kat knew something was wrong.

Like a traveler who wakes momentarily confused, she floated there, bobbing in the dark, holding her breath, listening, thinking, wondering what was different.

She tugged the strip of canvas that tethered her to the wall and pulled open the velcro clasp. As she drifted free she grasped onto a handhold next to the tether and swung herself round in the darkness. A green panel should have been softly glowing in the wall below the handhold, but she could see none. In fact, she realized, the cabin's darkness was absolute, without any of the little lights that usually were scattered around the room, softly glowing or blinking.

But still, that wasn't what had woken her.

There was something else....

Kat ran her hand over the wall, feeling for the green panel. She found it and pressed it deliberately. Normally, the touch of her hand would have illuminated cabin lights while gently activating the cabin's gravity, but the lights stayed off and Kat continued to float gently, and it was then that she realized what had woken her: the sound of silence.

Nothing. No jitters, rumbles or groans from the ship's superstructure. No thrumming from the power plant, no whisper of ventilated air or subsonic humming from the myriad machines built into her room.

At the realization, hair stood up on the back of her neck.

Absolute quiet is one thing you never want on a space ship.

Absolute quiet means death.

I wonder how long life support has been down, she thought quickly. She sniffed the air: it smelled fresh. And it was still pleasantly warm in her cabin. *I must have woken when it went out. Still, no time to waste.*

Kat calculated for a minute, orienting herself, then pushed off gently from the wall and felt herself floating in the darkness. She had no frame of reference and limply held her out her arms, ready to catch onto the approaching wall. She made contact — *feels like the closet door* — and gently settled to a stop.

Gripping a small protrusion on the wall, Kat held herself in place while opening the closet. She ferreted around for a moment and grunted in satisfaction as her fingers closed around her glasses. She was very glad now that she'd found this pair of Slimlines on Regis 5.

The Slimline Corporation produced the finest wearable electronics in the galaxy. What looked like a pair of stylish, simple eyeglasses was actually a quantum computer, complete with optical arrays and numerous sensors mounted invisibly in the frame, sensitive to voice or motion commands, bulletproof and virtually indestructible. This particular pair was equipped with an expensive option: the lenses were made of smartglass, a feature that provided the user with countless optical filtering and visual enhancements.

Slimlines were quite rare; only a few dozen were made. That alone made them very expensive. And the demanding craftsmanship required to design such a powerful machine without betraying its function in its form carried its own high price. The amount the Trader had quoted had made Kat gasp; nonetheless, she had willingly emptied her bank account to meet his demand.

Well, here's where I get my money's worth.

As she put on the glasses, they measured the ambient light and automatically switched on in full night vision, adjusting the colour spectrum to appear normal to human eyesight.

The room sprang to life and Kat, hanging upside-down on the wall, was momentarily seized by vertigo, then with a mental shift she reoriented herself and looked down into the closet.

She spotted her magnetic boots, spun round, pushed herself down to them and slipped in her feet.

After tapping her front teeth together once, she said softly, "Set boots to quick shutoff mode."

The Slimlines continuously monitored all her facial movements, and Kat had already programmed in her favourite few sequences. If necessary she could operate her glasses without betraying their use, with slight movements that were imperceptible to an observer. She could even choose to select icons off a virtual desktop simply by moving her eyes: the computer would track the movements of her retina. Mostly, though, she found it easier just to talk to it.

For now she forgot about her glasses as she quickly moved over to the closet where her spacesuit was hung. The Slimlines monitored the pressure and movement sensors in the magnetic boots and adjusted their levels over 300 times a second; if Kat suddenly broke into a run the boots would compensate every bit as fast as she could move.

She looked down nervously at a small package securely strapped to her sternum, just between her breasts, then pulled out of the closet a spongy, leathery bodysuit which she proceeded to squeeze into, a feat requiring catlike agility in zero gravity. She kept one boot on while she twisted and pulled her other leg into the suit, and then switched legs to finish the operation.

Soft magnetic cuffs at the ankles and wrists clamped seamlessly around matching cuffs on her boots and gloves, and a similar ring around the neck met its match in the suit helmet, a spacious, crystal clear Softdome. Her helmet provided unlimited visibility and was roomy enough to accommodate the Slimlines.

Kat was fully dressed in three minutes, but a quick check revealed less than 20 minutes of air in reserve; these suits were designed for quick transit, not long-term occupancy. If she intended on breathing for longer than 20 minutes, she needed to find another source of oxygen.

Kat told the Slimlines to run a full suit check and to advise her of anything pressing. She moved to her cabin door, released the pressure lock, and stepped into the silent corridor outside her room.

EROME KNEW right away when the power died because he had been expecting it. Well, if not a power outage specifically, then something equally sinister. He'd known that no good would come from the silent, late night arrival of a speeder ship, running dark and docking next to the Captain's quarters instead of at the usual visitors' ports.

There had been whispers among a few of the other crewmen for a couple of days, but Jerome hadn't been able to overhear anything meaningful, and no one was rushing to let him in on it. So he'd kept to himself and stayed ready for anything.

That morning, the tip-off had come when tightfisted old Captain Billarus gave shore leave to all hands without first trying to extort unpaid overtime and triple shifts from the worn-out spacers. Passengers wouldn't be boarding until tomorrow, and it hadn't taken long for Jerome to add two and two; whatever dirty work was afoot, prying eyes were definitely not welcome. It was exactly the kind of private party that he liked to crash.

Showtime, he thought as the lights died and the gravity faded away — although he hadn't expected such overkill: to lose gravity shipwide was a royal pain in the ass for everyone, and there were so many more elegant methods for most tasks.

But he already had a suit on, so he was hardly inconvenienced. As the last of the cabin gravity faded away his boots compensated; like a true spacer, he barely noticed the difference.

What a difference twelve years makes. In my first life, zeegee would have knocked me helpless as a kitten.

He snapped the suit's helmet onto his collar and activated the visor; his cabin sprang into blurry green life in the flickering display.

Jerome stepped ponderously over to a footlocker in the corner, clumping in a stilted fashion as the primitive computer in his ancient suit struggled to keep up with his movements.

He bent over and retrieved a small package, pressing it against his chest until he heard the soft click of magnetic clips taking hold; he then grasped two recessed handholds in the sides of the footlocker, pressed a small latch with his thumb, and pulled. The footlocker seemed to move up off the floor that it was bolted onto as its false bottom came clear of the box to reveal a shiny hand blaster velcroed to the base.

Jerome tossed the false shelf to the side, taking no note as its contents splayed out through the cabin in a psychedelic, zeegee arc. He slapped the pistol against his thigh and the velcro took hold.

Looking up just as his toothbrush floated by, glowing ghostly grass green before his face, he paused for a moment, shrugged (a pointless gesture in a space suit), then grabbed the toothbrush and stuffed it down into a side pocket on his suit.

So many habits too old to forget. So much worthless knowledge and useless skill.

Jerome tongued a switch in his helmet and waited while his boots slowly cycled down until he began to float up off the deck. He pushed himself over to the small bathroom, floated up to the ceiling, and pressed a small latch in the tile above the shower.

A section about two feet square popped free and Jerome peered into the conduit above it. The darkness was complete; the conduit was secure.

With a grunt he squeezed into the conduit, only slightly larger than the opening in the ceiling. He would have more room in the main line, about twenty meters ahead, but for now he'd have to painstakingly worm his way through.

Pulling himself along gently in the silence, Jerome was reminded of the first forty-some years of his second life: he'd been left floating in the darkness, looking for all the world like he was sound asleep, but churning madly in his mind, helpless to break free, yearning for one precious breath of air.

Jerome remembered vividly the expression on the scientist's face when he'd looked up into her eyes and said, "Good morning, doctor. How long have I been out?"

She'd expected inchoate babble, gibbered invectives and spittle flying from his lips.

But Jerome had just lain there, smiling, waiting politely for an answer to his query.

In later inquiries, the scientists were incapable of explaining their actions, aghast as one of their experiments had risen from the lab table to confront them in their cruelty.

How could they confess that they had revived him only for the sake of research, when the only humane action would have been to quietly cut the power and let him drift off into merciful peace?

Jerome felt a bump against his helmet and he twisted to the side as the main conduit opened before him. There was room here to stand up and he did so gratefully.

Deactivating his visor, he peered through the darkness for signs of life, and at the far end to his right he spotted what looked like tiny blinking stars. Someone was moving around down there and not being very discreet, carelessly using full spectrum light.

They must be pretty confident. Overconfident, I hope.

He kept his boots deactivated and pushed off against a support strut, sending himself floating quickly down towards the lights.

What Jerome needed most right now was information, and with his suit running on stealth mode, masking as much of his presence as it could, he was perfectly placed for a little surveillance.

If they were pirates, they wouldn't have bothered killing the gravity – pirates were more efficient than that. No, there was something else at stake here.

He pulled up to where the dots of light seeped in through the service panels. They were coming from two men noisily clumping along the corridor beneath the panel. Jerome slowed his pace to match theirs and cycled his suit's comm frequencies, hoping they were using an unencrypted short-range frequency. Their conversation suddenly burst to life in his head, causing him to start in surprise.

"— was supposed to be simple. All we had to do was grab a girl!" said a voice, rough and coarse in its inflection.

"Don't be an idiot, Delvon. When you heard the pay you should have figured this wouldn't be so simple. No girl in the universe is worth that much," said a second voice, milder than the first, but still bearing the harsh tone indicative of vocal cords seared from years of breathing cheap canned air. *Career spacers*, thought Jerome.

"So I'm greedy *and* stupid. They don't put you to death for that. But this is different."

"Yeah, I gotta admit, I never expected it'd go this far. When Robbie whacked the Captain it suddenly got real serious."

"All the more reason not to waste our time dealing with Robbie. As far as I'm concerned, our contract ended the moment the Captain's brains exited his skull. I heard what the boss told Robbie – the girl's not important, it's what she's carrying."

"And how does that help us?" said the second voice.

"So, moron, it means we make ourselves a new contract. And we keep it simple, which means when we find this girl we kill her and take whatever she's carrying. We cut out Robbie, deal directly with the boss, and opt for early retirement."

"And you expect Robbie just to stand back and let you cut him out of the action?"

"I'm betting Robbie won't have much to say about it with a piracy rap on his head and a hole in his brain," replied Delvon in a low growl. "Otherwise, our 'early retirement' may come a lot sooner than we want."

So they've killed the Captain. Jerome whistled silently. *What's so big they'd risk that kind of heat?*

Captains were inviolate. Langstrom Drive ships depended on skilled commanders, and to neglect to hunt down a Captain-killer would ruin the reputation of any serious transport company.

Jerome's thoughts were interrupted by a short squawk from a suit radio. All three men froze and listened.

"Shit, which way is that?" Jerome heard Delvon's voice, quieter now; the man was suddenly alert.

"Um, hold on a sec, I'm getting it on the heads-up… Section 5, Level 2, Cabin 18… there it is, down to the right."

There was a momentary pause while each studied the heads-up displays in their suit visors. "Okay, she's in the corridor, she should be easy to grab – just don't do anything stupid. I'll go first, you back me up."

Jerome heard none of the last of this, as he was already whizzing down through the conduit towards the location they'd mentioned. He didn't know what he'd do when he got there but he figured he'd be better off getting there first.

He peered back quickly and chuckled quietly as he saw the tiny pinholes of light veer off to the left; they'd taken a wrong turn. Things were looking up.

AS KAT STEPPED into the corridor outside her cabin, she reflexively glanced upwards. She knew there was a camera up there tracking her movements, but she wasn't sure if it was still operational.

While she could have jammed the signal, that would have done little more than send a homing beacon to anyone who might have been monitoring the system; for now she could only hope to pass unnoticed. Hopefully there was too much action elsewhere to make her movements worth anyone's attention.

She knew it was an empty hope, though.

She knew they were coming for her.

She should have expected as much, after running into the "prince" in the spaceport bar on the outer edge of the Kuiper belt.

Normally Kat wouldn't have gone anywhere near such a place while on a job, but it had been so long since she'd unwound, just relaxed.

After all, I'm not a machine, she'd reasoned, and the place was expensive enough to keep out all but the cream of society.

Or the biggest crooks, she realised now.

Either way, she'd noticed as soon as she walked in that she looked screamingly out of place. All her professional life she'd worked to cultivate an ordinary, nondescript appearance, but here it was her biggest giveaway – in this place "ordinary" was reserved for those with a lot to hide.

But foolishly, she'd stayed to get a drink and had almost lifted the glass to her lips when she felt his touch on her elbow as he slithered onto the barstool next to hers and introduced himself.

He was a small man dressed in cheap, dark clothing. Tiny, beady little eyes blinked rapidly beneath a pasty, mottled forehead that quickly receded into a wet gloss of oily darkness, perhaps hair. A thin, greasy moustache clung limply to his upper lip, the last feature on a chinless face that simply merged into his neck.

Prince of What, he didn't say, but Kat suspected it was Prince of Bullshit. She'd never seen real bullshit, but she knew its smell immediately when this smarmy con man opened his mouth. she wasn't taken in by his story but that availed her little: he discerned almost immediately that she was a Retriever, and the less she said the more interested he got.

"You know," said the little 'prince', weasel eyes darting around in his head as he examined Kat, "I could swear we've met before. I think it was… let me see, last year at Señor Guzman's ranch on Regis 5, wasn't it?"

"Sorry. I don't know that name," Kat answered dismissively, then knew she'd made a mistake. It was too late. The small man had picked up on her lapse; now he knew she was lying, and worse, probably suspected that she was indeed coming back from Regis 5.

No doubt he was using a voice stress analyzer, probably strapped on his wrist underneath his cheap clothing, delivering little coded pulses as it monitored his conversations.

She cursed inwardly and tried to remember her training: no direct answers, no lies, no truth. Questions, platitudes, nonsequiturs, but never answers! She must be tired indeed, to make such a childish mistake.

A Retriever heading back in from Regis 5 could mean only one thing: Discovery. A new planet had been discovered and it lay off the route through the most heavily traveled part of the settled star systems. That alone could make it worth untold billions of credits, and if it were M-Class, well, that kind of wealth could hardly be imagined. But the Discovery was worthless without the artifacts;

the little man knew he had uncovered only a small, but crucial, part of the puzzle.

Kat knew this, too, and gave up any hope of pretense.

"Well, I'm off, nice meeting you." She hoped his device revealed her lie.

Leaving her drink untouched, she hurried out of the bar.

The dark little man stood and watched her leave, then turned and angrily waved away the barmaid who had come to remove Kat's drink. He thought for a second, raised Kat's glass to his lips, swallowed the liquid, then hurried out of the bar in the direction she'd gone.

CHAPTER IV

THE PRINCE, or Nestor, as he was sometimes known, lost track of Kat in the spaceport, but he wasn't worried. He had a friend in Dispatch who was only too happy to trade Kat's travel information for a twenty-credit note; only twelve people had come aboard the spaceport in the last three hours, and Kat was one of them.

Nestor pored over her registered travel log – it looked for all the world like Kat had traveled to Omnos II last year, rented an apartment for seven months, and then decided to return to Earth. Typical Retriever pattern.

While a new planet could not be claimed without actual planetary artifacts returned, in person, to the Registration Board on Earth, that detail alone could not safeguard a Discovery for long. Once the location was known it was always possible to somehow delay the courier – *delay, or worse!* – until another Retrieval could be completed.

So Retrievers concealed their movements, traveling under many different identities, until they strode triumphantly into the Hall of Records to register their planet. The biggest companies hired only the best, for a careless or sloppy Retriever could jeopardize a find worth trillions.

And Nestor was *convinced* that Kat carried a Discovery of great value. A thrill shuddered through his body as he contemplated stealing the ultimate prize: the Real Deal, a planet capable of supporting human life! What a fitting way to wind up a career of fraud and extortion.

Nestor quickly scanned through Kat's log with the station Dispatch; he assumed all the information was false, so he ignored it, and instead looked to see where she was staying tonight – the ship's name would be near the end of the entry.

He spotted it: *The Pernicious*. An unlikely name for a starship, but then again, starships were strange affairs all on their own. The name probably fit. Departing for Earth in 65 hours.

Nestor hurried down to the spaceport ticket office and quickly booked passage on *The Pernicious*. He made two quick calls on the station's public phones, carefully paying in cash and declining to link his personal phone into the system.

In the next two days Nestor bribed the necessary crewmen, met with the Captain, and concluded all the deals he needed to snatch the girl and her Discovery in one lightning stroke. Robbie and his ship would arrive that night. An hour after that he would be speeding to Earth and about to become richer than Midas.

He settled into bed in his suite on the Pernicious, turned the gravity down to low, and drifted off to sleep.

NESTOR HAD TAKEN a cabin one deck below Kat's, and at the predetermined time he was out of his room, down the corridor, up the transit shaft, and quietly tapping into her door's keypad an override code he'd gotten from the Captain. When the door swung open he stepped inside and shot several tiny flechettes at the sleeping form tethered to the wall. After he was satisfied he'd hit his target he approached the body and spun it around to face him.

He cursed bitterly under his breath as a bundle of towels oozed out of the sleepsack. He'd almost expected this, but there had been no way to guard against it.

Time for Plan B. He sent a short, coded signal to his partners and exited the room. He was heading towards one of the shuttle bays when the gravity died along with all the other power systems.

I'm just dying to find out which moron decided to add this wrinkle, he thought bitterly as he flailed and bounced along the corridor. One of his magnetic boots was malfunctioning, and every few steps it would either yank his foot back down or push it out like a huge spring.

It was only after breaking his nose against a door frame and twisting his ankle that Nestor gave up, deactivated his boots, and clumsily pushed and pulled himself along in zeegee. Five minutes later he received a transmission from his confederates, and he spun off through the darkness toward the other shuttle bay.

CHAPTER VI

KAT NEVER SAW Nestor on board *The Pernicious*, and had hoped futilely that the little man was no threat to her. Until she'd woken up tonight, she'd almost convinced herself that she was just being overly paranoid. Now he was all she could think of as she looked right, then left, down the silent corridor.

She paused outside her cabin doorway. Silence. That was to be expected; as far as she knew, Kat was the only passenger on board. The ship wasn't departing for Earth until tomorrow afternoon, and those tourists who weren't partying on the Station were off on excursions to some of the icy planetesimals scattered through the Oort Cloud, squeezing in one last bit of day-tripping before reboarding for the jump back to Earth. The ship would be a frenzy of activity tomorrow as short-range shuttles descended en masse, filling the ship with chattering knots of humanity as they disgorged their cargo of interstellar sightseers.

But right now, Kat was alone.

OK, think girl. What kind of lead do we have on them?

Her thoughts churned frantically as she contemplated her course of action. A discreet numeric display in the corner of her vision showed 17 minutes of air left in her suit. There were shuttles on two decks. She called up the shortest route on her Slimlines, wheeled, and sprinted gracefully down the corridor to the pressure door.

"I'm picking up an encrypted burst from the Captain's Quarters," reported the Slimlines inside Kat's head. Miniscule speakers implanted into her ear canal provided her with perfect sound reproduction at volumes too faint for others to detect.

They know I'm gone; it won't be long now, thought Kat.

"Can you track the target?" she asked.

"Negative. They haven't responded yet."

"Well, tell me if you get a fix."

Kat fidgeted while the pressure door completed its cycle, alternately looking over her shoulder or peering down the corridor in front of her. She'd given up any pretense of stealth, knowing that her movements would long since have been picked up by any observers. She relied now on pure speed.

If they'd gone to her original cabin, then she had an advantage, but only a slight one.

Good thing she'd been paranoid enough to book a second cabin under an alias. She had considered booby-trapping the sleepsack, but a sudden vision of little bits of cabin steward scattered all over the room had tamed her plan.

The shuttle bay was at the end of the next corridor; it was possible her pursuers might not be able to beat her to it.

With a grimace, Kat saw through the door's viewport a figure burst into the transitway through an access port from a side corridor.

So much for the race, she thought as she grimly readied herself for combat. She quickly deactivated her boots and spun herself up and around, coming to rest against the bulkhead above the door.

The Slimlines were already jamming the corridor sensors and cameras. With any luck, her opponent would be unable to spot her before she could disable him.

The pressure door completed its cycle and silently swung open. Kat reached down from her position above the door and dropped a flash grenade into the corridor, just as a shower of flechettes streamed through the doorway and slammed harmlessly into the far wall.

She watched the flechettes pass by in crisp animation as the Slimlines reproduced the scene in visible images while protecting her from the burst of the grenade flash.

Instantly she swung through the doorway to confront the figure in the corridor staggering drunkenly and clutching at its faceplate. "Nice try, buddy. Too bad for you," she said as she stepped up to her would-be attacker and calmly shot a single flechette into his neck.

Her attacker stayed erect, swaying gently back and forth, still anchored securely to the deck by his magnetic boots, but all his other movements stopped. A bit of spittle floated lazily around inside the visor. His arms slowly floated upwards as his muscles relaxed.

Kat was already past him, fumbling madly at the controls for the door to the shuttle bay.

"Behind you, Kat," announced the Slimlines, but as she wheeled around she was slammed from behind and thrown into the bulkhead. Stars swum in her brain and she felt her arms hoisted above her head and pinned to the wall; she guessed a magnetic shackle had been applied.

"Hah. Not fast enough, baby!" crowed Delvon inside his suit. He looked over at his partner, swaying listlessly back and forth a few feet away. He hoped she hadn't killed him – this would be fodder for several years of ribbing. Caught flat-footed by a girl! Delvon chuckled at the thought. "End of the road, honey. Sorry it has to end this way." All his suit sensors were useless to him; *probably jammed by the girl,* he thought. He mimed a big kiss at Kat through his helmet visor and reached down to his thigh pocket and pulled out a long, sharp knife.

Delvon pushed back as the girl launched a kick at him, and regretted she couldn't hear him laughing. Suddenly, a blaze of white-hot pain ignited in his brain as his ears were assaulted by a train whistle in his suit helmet. The feedback from a thousand microphones screamed a jet engine love song at volumes that would deafen God. He screamed in agony but couldn't hear himself over the ear-splitting howl. He wondered peripherally why his helmet visor didn't shatter from the sound. He didn't know how the girl was doing it, but he knew he had to stop her.

Desperately, he slashed downwards at Kat with his knife.

Kat watched the man stagger as the Slimlines took control of his suit functions and fed a wall of sound into his helmet; she saw him recoil and then her eyes widened in horror as he swung his arm upwards, then down at her chest with a huge, silver blade.

His arm hadn't completed even half the arc towards her chest when his body suddenly jerked backwards. A tiny pinhole appeared in the man's visor as a shower of helmet, brain and blood erupted from the back of his suit helmet.

His boots deactivated when his helmet's integrity was compromised, and he floated dreamily backwards in the corridor while a cascade of bodily fluids pumped out of his helmet, from both holes now, twisting and spreading throughout the space around him, fracturing into thousands of tiny droplets.

Kat felt a gentle touch on her wrists, then the release of pressure as the magnetic shackles were deactivated; when she felt the cuffs open she spun round, ready for whatever was coming next.

She looked up. Hanging upside-down from an open panel overhead was a suited figure, holding a weapon but not pointing it at her. The figure gestured to its helmet and Kat guessed at the meaning.

"Cycle comm frequencies. Line of sight. Link," she instructed the Slimlines.

A green light lit almost immediately in the corner of her vision.

"Thanks," she said to the figure. "Now what?"

"Now we get out of here," replied the suit from behind a pitch-black visor.

The figure dropped smoothly from the ceiling, spun off to the far end of the transitway, effortlessly pulled open the heavy pressure door and glided into the shuttle bay.

Kat watched it disappear, shrugged, and followed it in.

EROME CURSED inwardly as he dashed across the shuttle bay. Whatever he was involved in, he was knee-deep in it now. He hadn't wanted to kill. *Primal reflexes. Still too strong in my brain.*

I hope I'm on the right side here. It had seemed at the time the noble course of action, but he feared his judgement might be suspect.

Delvon and his partner hadn't taken a wrong turn: they'd set off on an intercept course, something so obvious that Jerome couldn't believe he'd missed it. *Getting too old to play these games.*

By time he had made it to the reported coordinates she was already gone, of course, but the trail of open pressure doors couldn't have made her route more obvious. He'd guessed immediately where she was headed, but hadn't managed to beat the other men.

Her voice in his helmet snapped him back to alertness.

"Could you let me in on the plan, do you think?" he heard. "Maybe tell me the next step?" He looked up at the girl, who had caught up and was running effortlessly alongside him. He glanced downwards at her boots – expensive snugfit suit, good equipment. He remembered the days when he could afford such luxuries. Long time ago.

"Sure. Step Two: we stay alive," he answered quickly.

Jerome ran up to the shuttle and yanked open a side bulkhead panel marked **EMERGENCY MANUAL ROUTING** in vivid red stenciling. He pulled a thin cable from his suit and jacked it into an interface port, waited for the shuttle to recognise his access, then spoke a short series of quiet commands.

"I'm routing this shuttle to leave in four minutes. We have exactly that long to get out of this bay without being incinerated. You have any problems with that?" he asked Kat.

She looked at him in disbelief. Her Slimlines could not pierce the impenetrable blackness of his visor; his voice gave her no clue to his intentions.

"I can't stay," she replied. "I'm dead if I don't leave on this shuttle."

"We're not staying, but we're not leaving on this shuttle, either. It's child's play to track this craft – but they may think we're desperate enough to use it. That will buy us the time we need.

"If you want to live, you'll have to trust me."

"Go ahead," she answered. "But I hope you know what you're doing."

"So do I."

The tenor of his voice surprised Kat. It was old, like her grandfather's. He had to be in his 70's, at least, but he moved like a gymnast. Some of these old spacers had really benefited from zeegee life.

A series of red lights lit on the shuttle's panel.

Jerome pulled his suit cable from the interface and sprinted to the far side of the bay. Bright red warning lights started flashing around them.

They ran up to the access door and Kat moved to go through it but Jerome held her back.

"No, they'll know if you go back out there," he warned, as he pulled the door shut and spun the handle. Then he turned to his left, ran a dozen paces, and paused for a moment.

Kat wondered what he was waiting for until she saw him leap upwards to a shielded access panel thirty feet above them.

She didn't have to wait for her boots to cycle down; they shut off instantaneously as she leapt upwards to meet him.

The panel was already floating free when she arrived, and Jerome gestured her through, then followed her and pulled the panel back into place. It clicked into position just as she felt the tremendous rumble of the shuttle bay doors swinging outwards as the shuttle taxied free of the ship.

"Where are we? What is this corridor?" she asked Jerome's retreating form heading down the conduit.

"Engineering and mechanical access conduits," he replied without turning around or slowing his passage.

Kat looked far down the conduit; it continued for at least twenty meters, and she could see openings for several side corridors scattered down its length. She thought for a moment, trying to puzzle out a discontinuity in her mind. She looked up suddenly.

"Where are the airlocks?"

Jerome barked out a short, sharp laugh.

"Yeah, go figure. I guess that means the pressure doors in the corridors are just window dressing to give the tourists a false sense of security. I'm shocked, I tell you, shocked! What is this world coming to?"

Jerome was already far down the conduit. Kat spun herself round in his direction, and pushed off into the darkness after him.

CHAPTER VIII

NESTOR WAS CONFUSED.

He contemplated the scarlet cloud floating in the corridor, gently pulsing from Delvon's limp form.

The girl's escape had been completely unexpected, as unexpected as the sudden introduction of her mysterious confederate.

He was certain the girl was flying solo. Then how to explain this sudden apparition? A competitor? Perhaps. *But her competitor or mine?* Had one of the men he'd hired gone into business for himself?

Before he could make up his mind, the two were gone through the pressure door into the shuttle bay.

Nestor had absolutely no intention of involving himself in any pistol fights – the mere idea of it made him shudder – and he immediately abandoned any thought of pursuit. Instead, he turned and headed directly to the Captain's Quarters.

He was halfway there when he felt the rumble of the departing shuttle's engine. That made him hurry faster, almost tumbling onto his face as his sprained ankle caught a door.

The bridge, Captain's Quarters and engine room were located in a self-contained pod behind locked pressure doors. As Nestor approached, the pod doors recognized a microfilament in his suit and cycled open as he arrived.

As soon as Nestor passed into the pod, he plunged to the deck and smashed his face against his suit's faceplate. Gravity was still on in this unit. He staggered to his feet and tried to ignore the trickle of blood creeping down his forehead.

Halfway down the corridor he came up to a pair of sliding doors wedged open with a large wrench laid between them on the floor. Simple and effective. On the half-open doors he read:

APT AIN'
UAR TER

He squeezed sideways between the doors and entered into a scene of chaos. The floor was strewn with small objects, desk ornaments, memo disks, the kind of clutter seen only on planets or in environments where gravity never failed. *It must take an arrogant man to be a starship captain*, Nestor thought.

The Captain, or what was left of him, lay in a large pool of dark red liquid leaking from the back of his head onto an equally scarlet Persian carpet.

At the far end of the room, behind a large metal desk strewn with papers, two men in silver pressure suits were engaged in violent argument, screaming and gesturing at one another. Their helmets were off, but Nestor's was still firmly fastened to his suit, so to him the scene appeared as a dizzy pantomime. He unsnapped his helmet and as the seal released, their argument popped to life in his ears.

"Well I don't give a crap what you think of me, just so long as you remember this is *my* operation! You do what I say!"

"This is not the operation that I signed on for! You never mentioned piracy and murder!"

"I'm mentioning them now, OK? You have an objection, let's hear it!"

Nestor thought the time was ripe to make his presence known. "May I ask a question first?" he interjected gently.

His voice startled both men. They jerked around to face him.

"My name," he said, "Is Nestor, and I believe you work for me.

"And my question is: 'Who killed the Captain?'"

The figure on the left, a large, broad-shouldered man, even larger in his pressure suit, moved towards Nestor and extended his right hand. Nestor extended his own to the man.

"Name's Robbie, Mr. Nestor, sir, Charles Robbie, owner and Captain of *The Happy Robbie*, starship fourth class, and –" here he gestured dismissively at the man he had been arguing with – "First Mate Sloan Travis. And as for the late Captain Billarus, well, things just weren't working out with him, is all, so I decided –"

What exactly Charles Robbie decided will never be known, as he suddenly stopped talking, no doubt to allow his life force to exit his body unimpeded. Nestor lowered his hand, a wisp of smoke trailing from the tip of the small weapon he cradled in his palm.

"*Captain* Travis," he addressed the other man, calmly turning to face him, but significantly holding his right hand in a conspicuous position, "Have you been able to track the shuttle that just left?"

The other suited man drew himself erect and crisply replied, "Sir. We're working on it, sir, but so far we can't pick up hide nor hair of them, sir. Mostly we were trying to decide how to proceed next, sir."

"Well, allow me to help you out on that front. You will immediately recall any of your men still on this starship and return to your craft...."

Nestor continued with his instructions while the other man contemplated Robbie's prone shape, now laying crumpled on the carpet next to the former Captain Billarus, and wondered why he himself hadn't done that very thing to Charles Robbie months ago.

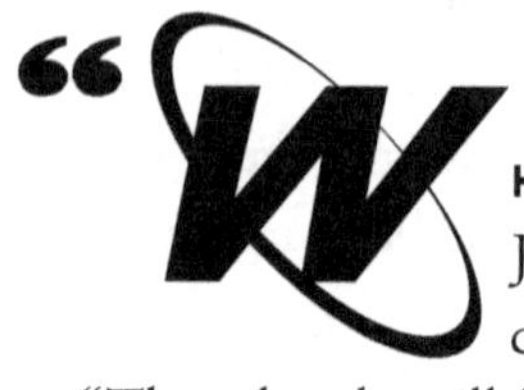**HERE ARE YOU** going?" called Kat after Jerome's retreating form down a side conduit. "The other shuttle's this way."

"That shuttle will be useless to us now. If it's suicide you're after, go right down."

"But I told you I have to get off this ship. <u>Now.</u>"

"And I *told* you we're getting off, but not in a shuttle."

"OK, so let's explore all our options… Let's see: can't use either of the only two shuttles… oh, hey – that's all there is. Unless you have a ship in your pocket, of course…."

"As a matter of fact," said Jerome, prying studiously at an insulated panel at his feet, then suddenly finding its latch and pulling it free, "I do."

Kat peered down into a large warehouse section. There was a dim shape filling the far end.

"Ladies and gentlemen, welcome to Cargo Bay 14," announced Jerome in his best tour-guide intonations.

"And this –" he took Kat's hand and pulled her down from the access shaft, "Is *The Time Lapse*."

Gently floating down from the ceiling, Kat cycled her Slimlines up and focused on the ship sitting among various large crates and assorted mechanical parts.

It was old. Not heirloom old, or even nostalgic old; just old like your parents' couch, out of style, yearbook photo haircut. It looked even worse in natural light, she discovered, as Jerome activated the ship's running lights and the Cargo Bay came to life in ghostly shadow.

"This is a piece of crap," said Kat in disgust. "It's cheap equipment, poorly designed and manufactured in haste. It's probably illegal to still fly one of these."

"Maybe," came the reply, "But it runs, and no one else knows it's here, except for the Captain, and he's dead."

At hearing this, Kat looked over sharply at Jerome. She was confronted by the blank canvas of his visor.

"God, would you clear your faceplate? I'd like to know what you look like."

"Oh – sorry. After that flash-bang you tossed out earlier, I wasn't taking any chances. Hold on…."

His visor suddenly snapped transparent. Kat smiled broadly and blurted, "Why, you're just a kid! What are you – 18? 20? And here I'd thought you were the Old Man of Space!"

"Yeah," replied Jerome, "The vocal cords never quite came back."

He saw Kat's puzzled expression.

"Regeneration. I was renewed."

Kat didn't say a word. She didn't know what to say.

What *do* you say to someone who's died and been born all over again – 'How was the trip?'

"Well… you look great. Ah – how – how old –"

"Almost 230, if you count the time in the tube."

Silence filled their helmets again. They could hear their own breathing.

Jerome felt the need to fill the quiet; he was used to this reaction whenever someone found out.

"But this ship," he ran his gloved hand lovingly along the hull, "Is positively a spring chicken compared to me, and I already saved your life once today.

"Let's see what she can do."

AN ICY DROP of liquid nitrogen grew silently on the O-ring, slightly frosting the refueling nozzle. "We've got a loose seal here," Kat called out, then quickly reached down and spun the valve handle on the portable nitrogen tank hooked up to the ship.

Jerome popped his head out of the small ship's belly and looked up at her. "Which?"

"Nitro."

"No big deal. It only leaks when you refill it. Close it tight when you're done, is all."

Kat rolled her eyes skyward. "I can't believe this."

Jerome dropped down out from the underside of the ship and snapped a panel back into place where he had been working.

"Everything loaded up?"

"Why exactly are we taking all this junk, again?" she asked, pushing the bulky nitrogen tank, now disconnected, through a cargo door in the small ship.

"One: it's not junk; it's the collected booty from twelve years of cut-throat trading and ruthless wheeling and dealing.

"Two: it's all I've got. If I throw it out, I've got nothing." The statement sounded pathetic to Kat, and she looked over at him sadly.

"Surely in 230 years you've accumulated a little more than just" – she glanced down at the label on a box, before pushing it in behind the tank of nitro – "than just 'FIFTY LITERS POWDERED GOAT'S MILK, BEST BEFORE 2225'...."

"OK," replied Jerome, "So not everything's worth its weight in gold. That doesn't mean we should throw it out. Some of these supplies are quite valuable on the remote mining stations, and until I unload them for a profit, I'm keeping them. Like it or not."

"Besides," he continued, "In 230 years I *did* manage to accumulate a little more than this –" his eyes swept sadly across the boxes and equipment scattered around them – "I just couldn't hold on to it, that's all…."

"Yeah, so what's the story there," asked Kat, lining up a series of small boxes in a twisting row, each floating and rotating just slightly out of synch with the others, gently colliding together and disappearing into the ship, one by one, as Kat directed their passage with small, deft taps to the hindmost box.

"I thought only the richest birds tried regeneration. Wasn't it super expensive? You didn't blow your whole wad on it, did you?"

"Yes, it was expensive, but still cost only a fraction of what I was worth. No, my wealth was lost to a much older, more traditional path: simple human dishonesty.

"I thought I would be under for only a few months, but once the lawyers got their hands on my money, greed replaced loyalty and they kept me frozen for several decades."

Jerome heard Kat gasp quietly but he didn't so much as pause; he was used to the reaction.

"Only problem is, no one had the guts to pull the plug and let me go gracefully. So, partly in the spirit of scientific experimentation, but mostly to remove for good a bothersome reminder of their past misdeeds, the decision was made to revive me.

"They didn't even bother trying to cover their tracks, they were so sure I'd be a vegetable."

A grim smile appeared on his lips as he recalled the event.

"That almost made it all worthwhile, seeing them stutter and panic when I confronted them. But they recovered fast enough, and I soon realized what most humans learn early on in life: f you have no money, you won't get far. They threw me out of their offices. I never recovered a penny."

"So what did you do?"

"The only thing I could do – I dug up a box I'd buried with money in it –" he caught Kat's surprised expression and chuckled. "Yes, people still do such things. Bought the best ship I could afford," his eyes flickered momentarily over to *The Time Lapse*, "And hunted down the son of one of my oldest employees. Asked him if I could store my ship on his passenger cruiser and work as a deck hand."

"Captain Billarus."

"There you go. And I've been trading ever since. Going on twelve years now."

"**O! M**USTN'T FORGET this," Jerome called out, directing a small, brightly-coloured box at Kat. She stretched out her arm and snagged a small rectangular carton that came drifting out of the storage bin that Jerome was rooting through.

On two sides of the carton was a distinctive green logo: a wide, three-pointed leaf superimposed over the old United States flag. The only other marking was a line of angry red lettering stenciled across the box that read **VACCINE REQUIRED**.

"OK, I give up. What is this supposed to be?" asked Kat, turning the box over in her hands, examining it carefully.

"Another consequence of sleeping through fifty years of social engineering," he replied. "One of my first experiences in this brave new world involved buying 5 cases of government-produced marijuana, 100% legal, guaranteed to get you high, but only if you had been properly vaccinated by a licensed physician."

"It was one in a series of Earth governments' greedy attempts to cash in on the drug trade, all the while still proclaiming that they were protecting us from ourselves."

"If you were to smoke this stuff," he said, taking the carton in his hand and pulling open the end flap, "It would make you so sick you'd retch uncontrollably until you passed out. Unless you'd been vaccinated. Of course, to get vaccinated you had to be over 21, and it required registration and hefty fees, both of which were taxed, to boot. You can guess what happened."

"People started selling black market vaccine instead of dope."

"Bingo. And to top it all off, the reefers didn't even get you very high. The vaccine sort of killed that part, too. The stuff was worthless within a couple of years of its release, but you couldn't know that if you'd slept through the last half century."

"So you got suckered into buying five cases."

"Why not? I was a smuggler. Just not a very good one."

"Did you at least get a supply of vaccine with it?"

"Of course. I said I was uninformed, not stupid."

CHAPTER XII

NESTOR SAT at the viewport in the captain's quarters and watched *The Happy Robbie* shimmer away in pursuit of the shuttle. He suspected it would be a long, tedious search. They had picked up no trace of the shuttle's signature on their sensors — either the craft had been destroyed or it was equipped with stealth devices. Unusual for shuttlecraft, but who knows what hijinx the late Captain Billarus had been up to. They were hunting for a needle in a haystack, but the effort had to be made; checking the nearest dozen or so spaceports would eventually produce a sighting, or maybe even the craft itself.

He sighed heavily. This was all going very badly.

Happily, the ship hadn't been registered in Captain Robbie's name, despite his braggadocio; in fact, *The Happy Robbie* wasn't even its registered name. It was a numbered ship owned by several numbered corporations registered with a numbered space consortium. Its true owner would never be found, and even if he were, he was dead anyways. Interstellar bureaucracy at its finest.

It had been a worthwhile effort to book passage in Robbie's name on this ship, Nestor thought smugly – *hopefully the investigators will be anxious enough to put paid to this unhappy affair that they'll accept unquestioningly the hypothesis of Robbie as a murderous passenger.*

He'd made sure both men who'd attacked Kat in the corridor were dead. *Let them be implicated in a mutinous plot – all the better to draw attention away from me!*

Travis should be back in a few hours, docking quite openly as a legitimate visitor, and Nestor would leave on the small ship and disappear forever. Even if the investigators did suspect something, he was just one passenger among many, one false name lost in the shuffle of interstellar travel, impossible to hunt down. With any luck, the missing shuttle would be the Number One target for any searches.

He sighed sadly at the thought of losing track of the Retriever. So close! His last chance for a lifetime of leisure, gone in a shimmer of light. He winced at the thought of returning to his interstellar bar haunts, cheap two-bit cons pulled on cheap, two-bit tourists.

I am worth so much more!

The Scotch in Nestor's glass wobbled slightly, a tiny ripple pulsing across the amber surface. He looked up in surprise – that was no visiting craft docking, it was the vibration of the ship's superstructure. A thunderous rumble that could indicate only one thing: someone was opening the hull!

Nestor ran over to the Captain's console and punched at the controls. The desk groaned deeply as its internal backup power supply kicked into active mode. The display stayed dark for a few seconds as the system woke up and retrieved current ship's stats.

Nestor snapped his fingers impatiently. He swore in frustration at the late, inept Charles Robbie, who had disabled the ship's primary power systems in a panicked attempt to flush the girl from her cabin, after the Captain had died protesting his ignorance of her actual whereabouts.

The information finally scrolled across the display: Cargo Bay 14 reported commands from an internal vessel, opening the bay doors, releasing one craft.

He raced back to the viewport in time to see a section of space shimmer briefly, and then snap back into focus as the small ship within it popped out of sight.

He jumped in place as he clapped his hands together excitedly.

All was not lost!

"**Y**OU SEE?**"** Jerome's smile of self-satisfaction was an almost tangible part of his voice. "I told you we'd have no problems."

Kat didn't look up: she was intently studying the star charts that flashed across the uppermost display. She answered without taking her eyes away from the dense rows of figures and calculations that scrolled rapidly down the screen. "Have you thought about what we're going to do when we drop out of interstellar mode?"

"They won't be looking for us. I've got that covered already. The shuttle we sent out was programmed for full shutdown concurrent with the completion of its jump.

"No one will be able to track it until it restarts. Ergo: never, baby. And until they find the shuttle no one will ever think to look for us in another ship. Face it: the perfect crime, thank you very much."

Kat turned away from the star charts and painfully looked up at Jerome. The Male Ego was so predictably overconfident.

She pulled back a strand of hair that had fallen across her face; large green eyes sparkled from behind the polarized shield of her Slimlines.

In the heat of the tiny cabin they'd both shucked their pressure suits in favour of thin body suits that clung to them tightly, lightweight clothing that did little to hide one's physical characteristics. Muscles rippled across Kat's back and arms as she twisted and contorted her body through the narrow confines of the pilot's station.

Jerome watched appreciatively, small beads of perspiration appearing on his forehead. Kat tucked two very long, very smooth legs beneath her and settled down into the webbing.

Kat noticed the attention she was receiving and chuckled inwardly. She hoped she hadn't been as obvious when Jerome had stepped out of his pressure suit. It had taken great force of will not to appreciatively run her hands down a bicep or across his chest. Spacers simply didn't look that good, not at any age.

For now, though, she forcibly drew back her attention to the task at hand.

"Listen, Genius, it's not that easy. Someone noticed us leaving, you can bet your booties on that. Now it's a race, is all."

"Then dare I ask where we're racing to?" Jerome asked. "I think I've earned at least a cursory explanation."

Kat sighed in resignation and took a deep breath. Jerome was right: he deserved to know what he was up against.

"I'm a Retriever."

Jerome pursed his lips in a silent whistle.

"Is it…" Jerome searched for diplomatic wording, "A… good find?"

"M-Class."

"We'd better get working, then. They won't be far behind."

KAT'S INITIAL impression had been bang-on: *The Time Lapse*'s better days – what few it had seen – were long past. Within a half-hour the ship's systems began to fail, one by one. Soon they had dropped into sub-light space to creep along under simple rocket power.

Jerome darted from console to console, fixing what he could, shutting down what was past repair. A few of the ship's systems could be adjusted using diagnostics programs from Kat's Slimlines, and she busied herself with these.

"It's hopeless," Jerome finally called out from behind a flickering panel. "The Drive regulator can't be repaired – we replace it or we can't control our thrust, it's as simple as that."

Kat looked up from the navigation displays and made a small movement with her jaw; the lights on the nav unit went dark. She took off her glasses and brushed her hair back from her forehead.

"It's funny, I didn't get the impression you were a quitter," she said, allowing a small half-smile to form on her lips.

"I didn't say anything about quitting. We just need to find a new part," replied Jerome, a bit testily.

"Oh, OK, that's different. We'll just pull up to the next repair station we come across and pick up a replacement… thrust regulator —"

"Drive regulator."

"— *Drive* regulator for a 20-year-old piece of flying garbage. I'm sure they'll have dozens in stock."

"You continue to amaze me with your perception, Kat. That's *exactly* what we're going to do."

He took her hand and led her over to the viewport.

"You see that little glimmer up to the right, about 2 o'clock? That's where we'll find the best repair yard in the Oort Cloud. We'll be there in about …" he looked over at the command console, "in about 3 hours, give or take."

Kat looked at him openmouthed.

"Well c'mon," he added, with a laugh, "You didn't think I chose this course at random, did you?"

KAT SWIRLED out of the way of a stray boot that was rotating toward her. She pushed off an overhead storage bin and sailed over to Jerome's side.

The failure of the ship's gravity systems had been more of a blessing than a curse, as it was infinitely more comfortable to move through the cramped cabin by floating than to step over and maneuver around the equipment bolted down throughout the craft.

A graceful pageant of small objects – souvenirs, tools, cans of food – swirled around Jerome's head, floating free of the cabinet as he searched the shelves. Kat hovered in place behind him, delicately plucking the tiny satellites out of the air and stuffing them into a webbed bag.

"Hey! Less velocity!" she hollered at Jerome as he tossed a small wooden cube over his shoulder. The block turned end over end in the air in a perfect intercept course with Kat's right eye. She caught the missile with an elegant swipe and held it up to her face. It was composed of tiny, movable coloured squares. She said delightedly, "I know what this is – it's a Rubik's Cube, isn't it?"

"Muh-huh…" came a muffled response from deep within the cabinet.

She looked over at Jerome and frowned. "Well, aren't you impressed I knew?" She didn't wait for a response. "So this is a primitive interactive puzzle. I bet you can do it. I've read about people like you."

This was all Jerome needed to pull himself out of the closet, spin himself around and fix her with what he hoped was his sternest expression. Only problem was, while he'd perfected this look by time he was sixty years old, he'd never considered how comical it might look on the face of a twenty-year-old man.

Kat tried not to giggle. To distract herself she tried to imagine Jerome as an old man, frail, wrinkled, bent over. The thought sent a creepy sensation rippling down her spine.

"Look," he began, taking a deep breath, "Do you have to talk like that? *'I've read about people like you.'* I feel like I should be sitting on a shelf in a jar of formaldehyde. I'm not a lab exhibit or a textbook case in 20th century social studies class.

"And secondly," he continued, picking up the pace, "Stop looking at me like –"

"Like what?"

"Like – like *that*. Like you're trying to find the zipper around my neck. What I did is no different from what millions of people do every day; I just did it all at once, is all."

"Millions of people do not seal themselves up in nitrogen and farm nanobots in their bloodstream!" Kat retorted.

"Neither did I! That's supermarket tabloid garbage!"

He checked himself mentally. "That is, that's just silly gossip.

"Would you like to know how it really worked?"

"On one condition," replied Kat. "I don't want to call you Jerome anymore. That's an old man name."

"And your point is….?"

"Sorry, but I can't treat you like an old man when you've got a body like that."

"So what can you call me?"

"How about… Jerry? That's a bit more youthful, isn't it?"

It had been too long since he'd been called Jerry. He'd left that moniker behind when he was barely sixteen, fearing it made him appear too young and immature, not to be reckoned with, not a serious person.

He thought a moment. Maybe now, after over two centuries of life, maybe he had finally come full circle and learned how to not take himself too seriously. "OK, it's a deal. Jerry it is."

Kat nodded. "Now," she said. "Tell me how it really worked."

"Well, it was all pretty straightforward. I went into the Clinic a very old man, one of the wealthiest in the nation, dying of pneumonia. As soon as I was pronounced clinically dead my body temperature was lowered and my blood artificially processed and pumped through my body. For the next two years every organ in my body was regrown from my DNA and implanted.

"The telomeres at the end of my cells were renewed, a dermal regenerator replaced my skin, and stem cells were removed from my brain, cloned, and reimplanted."

While he talked, Jerry twiddled aimlessly with the tiny replica of the Rubik's Cube; Jerry said it was a mini version he had pulled off a keychain he had once carried back on Earth, and he kept it now as a sort of lucky charm. Kat watched the interplay of the muscles and tendons along his forearms and tried to imagine them growing from a sick old man in a tube.

"The only unusual aspect to what I did was that, instead of going under for only a year or two, as should have been the case, I stayed under for almost half a century. The longer I was under, the more attached my estate's administrators became to my money and power. They stuck me in a cryo tube in the basement of some lab and left me to rot. After a few decades I was pretty-much forgotten.

"My original mistake was in waiting to be pronounced clinically dead before beginning the procedure; once I was "dead" I no longer had any rights as a person. I'm just exceedingly lucky that a curious scientist pushed her superiors to revive me to document my inevitable mental disintegration.

"The administrators took her up on it so they could finally get rid of me for good. Well, that was their plan, anyway."

"And now you're here," said Kat.

"And now I'm here, traveling through outer space in a tiny ship with a beautiful young woman.

"I'd say things worked out pretty well for me after all."

WATCHING THE dot in the viewport grow imperceptibly bigger left a lot of time to kill. They vaccinated themselves then broke open the Marijuanettes. Jerry was right – the most distinctive effect was a dull headache; at least it didn't last long. Then Jerry entertained Kat with magic tricks and some sleight of hand he had picked up while running 3-Card-Monte games on Fermis Prime.

Jerry knew a bit about how Retrievers worked and he asked Kat if she would show him the artifacts she was carrying to Earth.

Normally, Kat would have outright refused such a request but she surprised herself by readily agreeing, and she unzipped the top of her snugsuit and pulled out the little sack and handed it to Jerry.

It was a measure of her trust in Jerry, and, she reflected, an indication of the bond they were forming.

Jerry dumped out the contents of the sack into his hand and looked closely at them before pouring them back in and handing the pouch back to Kat.

"Pretty ordinary looking stuff," he said.

"Yeah, who'd guess they're worth a king's ransom?"

"Aren't you nervous keeping them on you all the time?"

"I'd be a whole lot more nervous if I left them anywhere. Until I get back to Earth, they don't leave my possession. You're the first person besides me who's ever seen or touched them. Hopefully the next person will be an Adjudicator on Earth in the Hall of Records."

"We should find a better way for you to keep them safe."

"If you're thinking about suggesting I swallow them or stick them up somewhere in my body, forget it, bub. They're fine where they are."

"Mm-hmm," said Jerry, but he didn't seem convinced.

Eventually the conversation turned to spaceship mechanics. Kat was surprisingly ignorant of how the machines worked. And to Jerry's astonishment, she lacked even the simplest understanding of the Langstrom Drive, the technology that made space travel possible.

"Did kids from your generation even go to school?" Jerry asked, exasperated.

"Oh, c'mon, my grandmother drove a car but she was no engineer."

"Mechanic."

"Whatever. Why don't you humour me and explain it?"

"OK, I'll do my best."

He thought for a moment. "Why do you think we have no cabin gravity when the Langstrom Drive is being repaired? The reason," he continued, without waiting for an answer, "Can be found in the Graviton Pulse Generator.

"In the thirties, Bob Langstrom was a scientist working for Bell Labs on a new mode of communication, a direct, instantaneous transmission that would pass through any barrier to find its target. His idea was to form a message of particles that are massless and travel at infinite speed.

"Now, when you're in the market for such quantum particles, your options are pretty limited.

"Aside from tachyons, whose existence we still can't verify, the only other choice is graviton particles, being both massless and able to travel faster than the speed of light. Even Einstein didn't completely understand how they work, and it took almost 150 years after they were first theorized before we could generate graviton particles in a lab.

"At that point, however, we couldn't control the flow of the gravitons; the early experiments were dangerous, unfocused forays into quantum forces.

"Langstrom's first hurdle was to design a graviton particle generator that wouldn't crush him or disintegrate the lab. He studied the literature from every graviton disaster and discovered the key: the gravitons could not be safely generated unless the machine focused the particle beam and directed it at an open area.

"Once he tried projecting them instead of containing them, the danger disappeared.

"That was his first breakthrough. Then he got cocky. He decided to develop a pulse of particles that he could beam as a binary message to a recipient. But when he tried to pulse the beam, he found that the particles tended to clump together into small pockets, making a coherent pattern impossible to discern.

"And one other thing bugged him: when he generated these "pockets" of graviton particles, they made loud "pops".

"Now, there was no apparent reason for the particles to make any noise: having no mass, they can't generate sound waves.

"As happens so often in the history of science, it was an accident that solved the mystery and led to mankind's greatest discovery. A short circuit on a power cell produced a small puff of smoke in the lab, but Langstrom was in the middle of a test run, so he ignored it and kept generating pockets of popping graviton pulses.

"That's when he saw it. In the smoke, as the particle beam passed through it, a swirling maelstrom of eddies. It was as though a giant drinking straw had been inserted into the smoke cloud and was drawing out puffs of smoke.

"Don't you see? That explained the popping: as the graviton pockets were formed in the smoke, they suddenly popped away, leaving a small vacuum in the smoke, each puff disappearing with a soft pop!

"Less than two days later, Bob Langstrom, working alone in his lab, designed the first prototype self-contained graviton pulse generator, a device that could produce a graviton pulse big enough to envelope the generator itself and transport it through space.

"In fact, a device very much like the device under our feet right at this instant. And I'll bet if Bob Langstrom were here right now, he could get it working again.

"In the meantime, though, we'll just have to content ourselves with simple thrusters. Wanna give me a back rub while we wait?"

CHAPTER XVII

KAT WATCHED the service station grow larger in the viewport until she could make out writing on the superstructure. At that point, she turned away and watched the ship's monitor track its approach.

The station must have software for every known craft, she surmised, considering that Jerry's ancient tub had linked in immediately. And once the ship was within 5 kilometers, the station took over completely, and efficiently ushered their ship in to an available bay in a repair section.

The repair bay was not large, with room for only three small ships, maybe four if they were parked nose-up. Huge overhead klieg lights stared down on the bay, but so many bulbs were burnt out that isolated puddles of light floated between swaths of greasy shadow. Coils of flexible pipe, cables, electrical wire and gas lines hung scattered throughout the repair bay, spilling out of access panels in the ceiling and walls.

One sparkling new ship perched on its hindquarters beneath a diagnostic array at the far end of the bay; eerie tendrils of mist or steam bled down from the belly of the ship, gathering into undulating clouds that almost completely obscured several men working there.

Jerry brought *The Time Lapse* to rest in one prominent pool of light surrounded by a red line painted on the floor; it marked out a huge rectangle, within which were painted the words, **GRAVITY HERE** . Despite the warning, Kat noticed as they taxied onto the spot, this spot was just as weightless as the rest of the bay.

"I've gotta tell you, Jerry, this doesn't look encouraging."

"Kat, haven't you learned yet not to judge a book by its cover? You, ah, do know what a book is, don't you…?"

He quickly ducked backward to dodge the shoe she threw at him.

Before their ship had fully come to rest, a door in one wall of the spaceport swung open and disgorged a fat man in the dirtiest pressure suit Kat had ever seen. He stood and looked carefully at their ship for a long moment, then turned and did something to a dial on the wall.

Kat felt the slightest tug, then a firmer pull, and then the sensation stabilized as about 20% Standard Earth Gravity settled in their craft.

"Not exactly breaking the bank on us, are they?" she muttered.

"Hey, they're here to make money, welcome to the real world," replied Jerry, moving over to the pressure hatch and punching the release sequence.

CHAPTER XVIII

~ 52 ~

ESTOR LEANED forward anxiously in his seat and peered through the mist swirling around the viewport. He watched while Kat and Jerry left *The Time Lapse* to disappear into the repair bay office with the fat man.

When the door closed behind them he suddenly exhaled, and was surprised to realize that he'd been holding his breath. Hours of waiting had taken their toll, and he was itching to grab his prize.

CHAPTER XIX

THE FAT man, whose name was Krupp, was both boss and owner, and managed only with great difficulty to restrain himself from salivating when he heard which part Jerry needed.

Sitting in his office, Kat tried not to choke on the stale air and stench of perspiration. Like gravity, air cost money, and Krupp spent only the barest minimum. Ventilation was virtually nonexistent in this cubbyhole – they were all probably inhaling the same air that the last twenty visitors had exhaled.

"You're in luck, Jerry," said the fat man, smiling broadly with all three chins.

"From the sound of that, I'd say you're the one who's feeling lucky right now," answered Jerry, also trying not to choke on the foul air.

The fat man, oblivious to the noxious environment, guffawed loudly at Jerry's remark.

"Haw! Maybe so, maybe so. But I'm not trying to go anywhere, and you are. And I happen to have the one part you need."

He paused for a moment to clean a blackened fingernail with his teeth.

"But even so, my price is fair."

He paused once again, to let the thought hang in the air.

And then, casually, "One thousand credits."

He said it as though the sum were an unimportant detail.

And Jerry, despite being prepared for the most egregious of robbery, blanched. For a moment, the only sound in the room was the click of Krupp's teeth as he chipped away at a particularly tenacious morsel snagged on his fingernail.

Then Jerry spoke.

"I – I can't possibly —"

"Deal." Kat's interruption cut Jerry off definitively.

"And twice that if you have it in my hand within five minutes," she added.

For a fat man, Krupp could move extremely fast. He was up and out of his chair, out a side door of his office, and back in the room, puffing, with a small brown box in his hand, three minutes later.

AS QUICKLY as Krupp moved, Kat was quicker. She had two glimmering banknotes laid on Krupp's desk and the box in her hand before the fat man could come up with any "surcharges". She grabbed Jerry's arm, turned, opened the office door, and walked straight into the chest portion of an armored pressure suit.

Captain Travis wrapped Kat up in a smothering bear hug and carried her back into the office, bowling over Jerry, right behind her.

As Jerry looked up from the floor, he saw Travis dump Kat into a chair, where she crumpled and sat motionless. Then Travis, pointing a hand weapon of some type, motioned to the other chair.

His meaning was clear and without a word of protest Jerry moved to the chair and sat down beside Kat.

Explanations were simply not needed. Everyone in the room immediately understood what was happening.

Travis looked at the floor and said quietly, to no one in particular, "We're sitting here, OK? The boss is on his way. So we're just going to wait until he arrives. OK?"

It wasn't a question, and nobody answered. They all just looked at each other, and listened to Krupp's tortured breathing.

Calmly then, Travis lifted his hand to his throat, touched a button, and said quietly, "You can come now. The area's secure."

AFTER TWO minutes of waiting in tense silence, everyone in the room started fidgeting. Travis started in on a truncated pacing pattern, moving two steps back and forth over and over like a tiger in a cage. Krupp drummed his fingers on his desk, Jerry's feet jiggled and tapped on the floor, and Kat – well, Kat moved nothing more than her eyes, carefully, assessing each person's movements.

"Hey, hey, watch it there, honey," objected Krupp, as Kat fiddled with a zippered pocket on the side of her snugsuit.

"Calm down, killer, I'm just looking for refreshments," Kat answered calmly, reaching into her pocket and slowly extracting a packet of Marijuanettes.

"See? They won't bite. Want one?" She popped the top off the pack and knocked a couple of reefers out of the carton, slipping one between her lips before holding the other out to Krupp.

"No thanks. Doesn't mix well with the nicotine."

Krupp reached into his own shirt pocket and pulled out a pack of illegal tobacco cigarettes.

"Suit yourself. Lend me a light, though, wouldja."

Krupp walked over to Kat and the two bent forward over a small gold lighter that flickered to life in his grease-stained fist, the air around their heads swirling with a turbulent cloud of smoke as they puffed their cigarettes alight.

"Aaaahhhhh, yeah, that's the trick...." Kat stretched luxuriously, slowly exhaling though her nose, letting the smoke bubble up around her face before the wash of air from the ceiling fan churned it into a quickly scattering cloud.

"How about you, Travis, wanna relax with me?"

Lazily, Kat twisted around and bent backwards in her chair, looking through a tumble of hair up at Travis, who stood close behind her, fidgeting uncomfortably.

She arched her back, letting the snugsuit accentuate the swell of her breasts. Pulling her legs up and around, she draped them over the arm of her chair, pointing her toes. A tiny bead of sweat glistened on Travis' brow; it seemed to him that the temperature level in the room rose slightly.

"No thank you, miss," he replied stiffly.

"You sure? You look like you need a break, honey, and I sure hate to smoke alone."

"Looks to me like you're doing just fine, miss," he answered, coughing slightly as Kat, giggling, blew a long, grey line of smoke in his face.

"Haw!" roared Krupp, choking in laughter, "Watch out, honey, we got ourselves a pink lung here!"

Kat giggled giddily along with Krupp and exhaled another long trail of smoke at Travis, then one at Krupp. For the next minute, giggling furiously, both alternated blowing smoke at one another and at Travis, roaring with hysterical laughter whenever he coughed.

CHAPTER XXII

NO **SENSE** *in being careless*, reflected Nestor. He'd had to force himself to stay hidden in his craft while Captain Travis grabbed the fugitives. Wouldn't be prudent to stick his neck out now; after all, that *is* why he had a payroll.

He'd briefly considered enlisting the help of some of the other crewmen, but decided that in this matter discretion was paramount. Travis was more than sufficient to carry out this task, and the fewer greedy minds knew about their mission, the better. As far as the crew were concerned, they were here only for maintenance, nothing else.

When the call came, Nestor took a deep breath and collected his thoughts, then selected a long serrated knife from the weapons locker and stepped out of his ship. He fell twice – *damned twisted ankle!* – and almost impaled himself on a robot welder, but within five minutes of getting the call he walked up to Krupp's office to face the Retriever once again.

He thought back to their previous meeting with an evil smile. This time, he reflected smugly, she wouldn't be leaving first.

As he opened the office door, he was almost knocked over by the wall of smoke and stale perspiration that blasted his face. He coughed and squinted his eyes against the fumes; he focused on the girl sitting in front of Travis, who was now nervously bobbing in place from side to side.

All the room's occupants looked up at Nestor as he entered. Kat almost snarled, but instead turned her eyes away and stared at her hands folded in her lap.

Slowly, Nestor circled the room, studying each of the captives carefully. Then he stopped in front of Kat. He gestured slightly, and Travis moved around behind Kat and grabbed her arms just below her shoulders, then wrenched her to her feet, holding her arms tightly to her sides.

Sneering, Nestor leaned closer, almost touching his nose to hers.

"Now let me see…" he began, twirling his blade slowly in one hand while the other reached out and stroked Kat's neck.

"If I were a cute-as-a-button little Retriever returning with my priceless find, where would *I* keep my precious package…."

His eyes raked tortuously down her body, and then back up again, lingering on her cleavage. Travis held Kat's arms tightly, pulling her elbows behind her back while she twisted viciously. Nestor pretended not to notice her struggles as he slowly bent over and pressed his face against her stomach, just beneath her breasts.

Suddenly, he pulled himself erect, stepped back a foot, and slashed down viciously at her sternum where his cheek had just rested.

At the movement of Nestor's blade, Jerry wrenched himself forward, screaming, only to be knocked backwards by Krupp's heavy fist slamming into his face.

He fell to the floor and looked up through a stream of blood to see Kat still standing, calmer now, her snugsuit split in two down to her waist, a small leather sack bulging incongruously from between the rise of her breasts. An angry red line down her chest and stomach below the sack betrayed the path Nestor's blade had taken.

"Now what have we here?" crowed Nestor. In his joy he couldn't completely restrain himself from dancing in glee, almost skipping in place, eyes glued to the package taped to Kat's sternum. Reaching out, he tore it off her skin with one violent sweep of his hand. Kat bucked furiously, then sagged back against her captor.

"Can it be?" he cackled. "Can it really be this easy to make a trillion credits? I'm almost scared to look inside!"

His eyes swiveled round to squint at Kat, crying now, jaw clenched, hissing, almost spitting out her breath between her teeth, holding Nestor in her gaze as if to memorize forever his hated face and foul sneer.

"Open it, Nestor!" shouted Travis, winded from restraining Kat. "Enough bluster! Open it now!"

His voice seemed to snap Nestor back to reality. Turning away from Kat, he strode over to the desk, yanked open the drawstring on the small sack and upended it.

Out onto the desk came tumbling the bag's contents – a small stone, a chunk of wood, packets of grass and a small, mummified creature, possibly a rodent.

The occupants of the room stood silent, staring at the tiny collection, the wealth of a nation, lying spread out before them.

The objects were pathetic, looking for all the world like nothing more than a child's souvenir collection from summer camp. Nothing in their presentation belied their true value. To anyone else they were garbage, but to these five people they were a lifetime of dreams.

For a moment, time stood still while each contemplated the value of the sack's contents.

Nestor was the first to snap back to life. Drawing his hand across the desk, he swept the artifacts back into the bag and pulled the drawstring tight. He straightened up and turned to look at Kat.

"It won't be more than a week or so before we backtrack your course, my dear. So that leaves us with the age-old question: 'What do we do with you?' We can't have you going off and telling tales of piracy, now can we?"

Nestor's triumphant sneer seemed to soften for a moment and he continued a little more softly. Jerry looked down and saw that Nestor's black blade was once again in his right hand.

"We'll have to kill you both, of course – can't be helped, don't you know…. Although I'm sure we could find something to do with *you*, my dear, for the next few days, no sense in throwing out such a pretty package right away…."

He didn't see Jerry coming. No one saw him coming. Without so much as a grunt he burst up and out at Nestor with the fury and force of a locomotive.

The explosion of his contact threw both men several feet across the room. The bag of artifacts skittered across the floor to Nestor's left and the dark black blade shot out of his grasp, skittering away to the right.

Without pausing, Jerry dove over to the right, stretched out, felt his fingers close around the grip of the knife, scrambled to his feet, spun around to confront Nestor, and tumbled backwards as a twenty-pound wrench smashed into the side of his skull.

He crumpled to the floor and lay motionless.

"That should cool his jets somewhat," muttered Krupp, hefting the wrench and slapping it down against his palm.

Tenderly, extending each limb gently as if checking for damage, Nestor drew himself back upright. He stepped over to the bag of artifacts and picked it up off the floor.

He quickly glanced over at Jerry's prone figure then turned to glare at Kat. He had to concentrate a moment to focus in on her; in the tackle he got from Jerry he might have hit his head, he worried.

He furrowed his brow and squinted closely at her. She was coming into focus now, but still seemed to be wavy and distorted.

He looked up in panic at Travis – he, too, appeared wavy and multi-dimensional.

Nestor snapped his head around to the left and looked at Krupp.

The man's head was swirling obscenely in a kaleidoscope of colour.

And then, while Nestor stared, goggle-eyed, Krupp seemed to disintegrate before his eyes, tumbling forward and smashing into the ground on his face.

Nestor turned and looked at Travis.

The man was swaying back and forth, still tightly gripping Kat but not so much to restrain her as simply trying to stay upright himself.

Drugs!

The thought exploded inside Nestor's brain.

He didn't know how, but somehow they had been drugged! He had to get away before he succumbed!

He leapt for the door and dashed down the dark corridor. He hit a zeegee path and flew, tumbling, spinning along the transitway until he came crashing into a huge, steel pressure door. His shoulder burned in pain where he'd struck and he felt his arm going numb.

Yanking the door open, fighting to keep his stomach contents within himself, he drunkenly threw himself over the threshold then pulled shut the door and snapped down the emergency latch.

That would keep anyone from opening the door, long enough for him to find a dark corner to curl up in, to vomit and pass out, away from hostile hands.

He staggered off into the dark, unlit passage, bouncing off walls and support struts like a human pinball.

There! An open door!

He flung himself through the doorway and slammed the door shut behind him. And the last conscious action he took before collapsing behind a row of crates was to look down at the little bag he clutched convulsively in his left hand.

No rips, no holes, the drawstring was tight; he loosened his grip only just long enough to squeeze the small lumps in the bag, thinking of the riches they would soon bring him.

While he still could, he yanked open a flap on his suit, stuffed the bag inside, and resealed the pocket.

Let the girl get away. Before she could even begin another trip to the planet he'd have registered the Discovery as his own. And then, when he had his billions, let her try to fight him. He'd crush her like a bug.

And with that thought, Nestor succumbed to the toxins pulsing through his system, doubled over, vomited, and passed out.

KAT FELT Travis going over and twisted free of his weakening grip to watch him collapse onto the deck. Before Travis had even hit the floor, though, she was already kneeling at Jerry's side, turning him over, slapping his face.

"Wake up, Jerry! Wake up!"

She slapped and shook him, pinched his cheek, pulled his hair.

Slowly, his eyes flickered open, he squinted, and then, remarkably, was instantly alert.

Forty years in a tube haven't slowed his mind, she reflected.

They were both on their feet and running for their ship as the first gurgling bursts came echoing after them across the repair bay.

"They'll be too busy vomiting to care about us for at least a half hour," said Jerry. "I see you weren't so panicked that you forgot to grab the Drive regulator."

"Or my money," grinned Kat, briefly flashing the two credit notes she'd liberated from Krupp before parting. "I'll be needing this to fund my next year of planet hunting. Still, I'm glad to escape with my life; I thought we were a done deal back there."

Jerry didn't respond, other than to grab the new part from Kat's hand and to leap into their ship. Within five minutes they were shimmering out of sight as they made the shift into light speed.

**HE WORST** thing about surviving a close shave is enduring the adrenaline crash that comes afterwards.

While their ship hummed through space on its preprogrammed course, Jerry and Kat lay collapsed on the deck, half-buried in piles of no longer weightless debris, each consumed in their own private reflections.

"God, I was *sooooo* close," moaned Kat. "Oh God, God, God...."

"Does it really mean that much to you?" asked Jerry. "I mean, you only work on commission, right? So it's not like you lost a trillion credits yourself – just the company? And we're both still alive, doesn't that make up for a lot?"

"Yeah, don't go there, OK? You can't imagine what this means to a Retriever. I'm not sure I wouldn't rather have stuck around and battled Nestor's goons to get that bag of artifacts back. If I hadn't been gambling your life, too, I probably would have."

"Well," replied Jerry, "It's awfully funny you mention gambling.... You *do* know how 3-Card-Monte works, right? And the skills you pick up when you run the game?"

Kat looked at Jerry with complete confusion, not understanding a thing.

IT TOOK almost three hours for Nestor to regain consciousness, and another ten minutes to wipe all the dried vomit off his face and arms. His head hurt worse than he would have thought possible, but despite it all, he was in an excellent mood.

Nothing could tarnish this victory, he reflected. Patting the small bulge in his suit pocket where he had the bag of artifacts, he almost broke into song. Oh, the sheer bliss of it! God, could life get any better?

He couldn't resist peeking at the artifacts once again, watching them tumble around in the palm of his hand – it would help him visualize the truckloads of banknotes they represented.

He loosened the drawstring on the leather pouch and shook out the tiny objects.

That Retriever had dosed him with some especially nasty drugs, he reflected abstractly. Why, in this dim light, with his brain and optic nerve addled by the aftereffects, the artifacts almost looked like a hex nut, a small bundle of shredded paper, and an ancient, souvenir Rubik's Cube.

hostages

JERRY FLEXED his hands, but the straps held fast. The men who'd tied him up had done a good job.

He looked around the small room; there was not much to see. The only feature on the far wall was a pressure door, such as those found on starships. A bright red LED glowing on the door's keypad indicated the clear message that the door was locked.

The room was spartan, to say the least. Aside from a metal bench bolted to the bulkhead, a large metal sink, and a wall of tall lockers, it was quite bare.

Jerry himself was bound tightly with velcro-type straps, and had been left lying on the floor. His right cheek, which rested against the decking, could feel a slight thrumming in the ship's superstructure – they were probably traveling at lightspeed, but he couldn't be sure; a starship could actually be more inert at lightspeed than when at rest.

"Well, no point lying around taking in the sights," he muttered. And instantly, he grimaced. Tentatively, he touched his lips with his tongue – they were sore, swollen, and cracked. A result of being beaten and left lying unconscious for… he pondered… how long *had* he been lying here, he wondered. No way to know.

Groaning, wincing, he painstakingly inchwormed himself to his knees, then to his feet. His arms felt numb, a consequence of being bound so tightly behind his back.

He stood in place, swaying slightly, pausing while a rush of blackness came over him, and then breathing in deeply as his vision slowly cleared and he caught his balance.

Now what?

Moving in comical little bunny hops, the best his tightly-tied ankles would allow, he examined the bench, hoping to spy a protrusion or sharp corner that he might snag on the straps binding him.

Nothing.

The seat was a single unit of molded metal, smooth, gently curved, designed to avoid catching on any gear that might brush against it.

The sink had no faucet, just a hole in the rim where water would pour out when a proximity sensor was tripped. Nothing to snag on there, either.

Jerry bent down and put his face in front of the hole; hot water spurted out and dripped red off his face, washing the dried blood off his lips and chin. He filled his mouth and spit.

Nasty. Recycled. Yuck.

When he leaned against the sink, he could feel Kat's Slimlines in his pocket, pressing against his hip. He regretted never having asked Kat to make him an authorized user; her computer would have really come in handy right about now.

He hopped over to the lockers; they were all locked and without protrusions. This cabin was a minimalist's paradise, he reflected.

Jerry flopped down onto the bench and pondered. Something in the back of his brain was nagging at him, something learned long, long ago….

He sighed, and closed his eyes. He wondered briefly how Kat was making out, then quickly pushed the thought from his mind.

He needed to focus.

CHAPTER II

KAT, AS LUCK would have it, was going through pretty-much the same struggle as Jerry.

She was sitting in darkness, in a small utility room. Her face hurt less than Jerry's, but she winced every time she breathed in. *Feels like a couple of my ribs are cracked.*

Other than that, I'm top o' the world.

Kat's room was different from Jerry's; hers was obviously an electrical or maintenance room of some kind. Banks of switches and thick cables lined the walls, humming, accented with an occasional flashing or glowing dot. Peaceful, ordered chaos. *Probably this deck's systems center,* she reflected.

Her hands were bound behind her, tied somehow to a post or pillar near the doorway. She was sitting on the floor, just out of reach of anything in the room.

Her captors had taken her clothing but thankfully had left her in her bra and underwear. Kat reflected sadly how men thought the best way to render women helpless was to deprive them of their clothing.

Like we're unable to fight back if our ass is showing.

Whatever lights there might have been in the room were not activated, but if her captors had left her in the darkness in hopes of disorienting her, they had not taken into account the small strip of light that glowed in the floor at the base of the door.

The designers of this starship had thoughtfully included light strips inside and outside every doorway. The strip in this room provided enough illumination to help Kat get a good look at her surroundings.

She squinted through the dim light at the largest array. Maybe life support, maybe gravity control; she couldn't tell – without her Slimlines, she wasn't very good at diagnosing equipment.

Jerry would know, she thought. *I guess I've been depending on him too much recently. Been neglecting my education.*

She turned to the other wall. Same stuff, just as inscrutable.

She sighed and sank back against the post. There would be time enough to sightsee when she was free.

She twisted her body to the right, crab-stepping her feet – *ouch! Damn ribs!* – over to the light strip in the floor. And then, raising her right leg above the strip, she started bashing the illuminated panel, over and over, as quietly as she could, with the heel of her bare foot.

CHAPTER III

IT HAD STARTED off innocently enough – a relaxing sightseeing trip around the six moons of Placido Domingo. Neither Jerry nor Kat spoke any Spanish nor had any Spanish friends, but that was the greatest appeal – an environment where no one knew them, where virtually no one could converse with them, where they could be left alone, in peace, with just each other to concentrate on.

The perfect place for a budding romance to take root.

And that was how it was working out, too, until a Placidan Customs officer on the fifth moon took a liking to Kat's Slimlines, a set of eyeglasses that discreetly incorporated a powerful quantum computer, and had decided to "confiscate" them for his own.

Now, anyone who knew Kat even slightly would have known better, but when you're a minor official on the outskirts of the galaxy, stuck in a go-nowhere position frisking drunken tourists, your judgment becomes the second casualty of your ruined career, right after your honesty.

Kat hadn't ever let anyone walk all over her. Five feet eight, possessed of iridescent green eyes and a lion's mane of shimmering red hair, a body to die for and an intellect just as deadly, Kat was no domesticated pussycat. She was an independent woman in one of the world's deadliest new professions: she was a Retriever.

Retrievers explored unknown space, staking claims for Earth's wealthiest corporations, all locked in a frenzied battle to "discover" and claim whatever usable planets, moons or even large asteroids could be found.

To be a Retriever meant living a life of subterfuge and deception, hiding your movements and concealing your finds until you could safely stake your claim in Earth's Hall of Records. Until that moment, however, a Retriever was Fair Game for all the crooks, con men and out-and-out thugs the galaxy could produce. No one cares who made the find – the only thing that matters is who stakes the claim.

The end result was a class of independent, fierce adventurers, trusting no one, often working alone for months or years at a time, resilient and resourceful. And Kat was one of the best.

And now, in her off-time (did such a thing even exist?), Kat was being hustled by this cheap, brutish Customs official.

He pretended he spoke no English. It made his theft harder to dispute. Instead, he babbled a rapid string of meaningless Spanish at Kat as he wagged his finger in her face, trying to give the impression that he had caught her with some horribly impermissible device, rebuking her as though she were a child.

Kat focused on the finger wagging in her face, as the official slyly (or so he probably believed) pocketed Kat's computer. It was just as her hand began the journey which would swiftly grasp the man's finger, snap it off, and jam it into his left nostril that Jerry grabbed her wrist, squeezed it firmly, and said in what he hoped was Spanish, "Ah, ah, scuza, er, yo dispachio… ah, OK?"

The official grinned. He perceived he had won. His left hand stayed in his jacket pocket, where it caressed Kat's glasses. His delight at his acquisition blinded him to the expression in Kat's eyes; had he looked more carefully, even his dulled senses might have perceived the folly of his action.

He wanted nothing more from them; in fact, he was anxious to see them leave. So Jerry obliged, and yanked Kat's wrist, and her body followed, and they stumbled down the gangway and into the spaceport on the God-forsaken fifth moon of Placido Domingo.

"**H**OW LONG, do you think, before he tries them out?" asked Kat nervously, stirring her drink for the thousandth time, eyes fixed on the masses of humanity surging though the spaceport.

Jerry lifted his eyes up from the table and furrowed his brow slightly. "I dunno. Something that good, he's probably itching to slip them on and fire 'em up for a test drive, but he's also probably terrified to have anyone see him with them – if his superiors see them, they'll grab them even faster than he did.

"No, he's probably got to wait until his shift ends, so he can get far away from all his coworkers, from anyone who'll see what he's got. And I don't think they're going off shift anytime soon."

Kat mulled this over. She trusted Jerry's opinion more than anyone else's. Not because she was falling in love with him, but because he was supremely qualified at assessing other human beings, having had over two centuries to hone his skills.

Jerry was a creature from another time, a man of the past. He had been rejuvenated in a tube after he had already lived more than his share of years. He had built corporations and run commercial empires that spanned the globe, but now, in his second life, with all his wealth lost to the sands of time and the evil of men's souls, he was just another spacer.

But he knew people better than anyone Kat had ever met before. He could judge a man's character by the grip in his handshake or the expression in his eyes. He often knew what Kat was thinking before she did, and he could manipulate, outthink and befuddle anyone who chose to match wits with him.

In short, he was the perfect partner for her.

They'd been thrown together by accident, each a participant in a deadly game of intrigue as Kat had raced to Earth to claim a new planet. And now, months later, they were still together, de facto partners in a business Kat had never thought she'd share with anyone.

Retrievers might be solitary creatures but Kat knew a good thing when she found one. She had no intention of letting Jerry get away from her, and she could tell that the feeling was mutual.

She'd taken time off after her last Retrieval, and she and Jerry were really starting to mesh. She loved the perspective he brought to modern life; he saw everything through the eyes of a visitor, no matter where they went. It was to be expected – he was a creature of a previous world. It wasn't just the forty-something years he'd spent in the regeneration tube; the almost two hundred years before that had been an equally cloistered existence.

Very Rich Men didn't live in the same world the rest of us do. Generations had passed since he'd shopped in stores or walked down a street. And now, everything he saw or did he approached with the curiosity of a child and the wisdom of a grandparent. It made for a bizarre experience.

That morning, as Kat and Jerry were waiting to disembark their sightseeing shuttle, Kat was watching news vids on her Slimlines while Jerry perused a news foil he'd bought at a vendor onboard.

"God, what a cesspool this system is," she muttered.

"Mmm?" replied Jerry, still scanning the foil.

"In just the last few days, the planet's refineries have been sabotaged by separatists – they don't say what they're separating from – and the Third Moon's CEO has been driven from office by a blackmail scandal, a "Princess Cassia" from this moon has been kidnapped, and the First Moon is being evacuated because of "abnormal" toxic emissions from its ore fab plants."

"So we're OK then," answered Jerry, not looking up.

"I'm sorry?" responded Kat. "You think all that's normal?"

Jerry finally lowered the news foil and looked up into Kat's green eyes. He smiled wryly. "Normal? By Earth standards, that's almost utopia."

Kat looked confused.

"When I was growing up…" began Jerry, invoking the familiar phrase that often prefaced their conversations, "Not a day would go by on Earth that the news wouldn't include stories of civil and international wars, environmental disasters, various pandemics, and corporate and government scandals. Kidnappings in some countries were so common they were almost a part of daily life, like getting your purse snatched or your bicycle stolen."

He stopped talking, noticing Kat's expression. "Oh, no, where did I lose you? Was it the purse reference or the bicycle one?"

Kat punched him in the arm. "Neither, Einstein." Even Kat knew who Einstein was; she knew of Edison and Henry Ford, too. Jerry made her watch a historical vid every day on her Slimlines.

"I just thought we'd made progress since the Stone Age, that's all."

"We have," answered Jerry, eyes twinkling. The "Stone Age" reference was a typical expression for Kat; Jerry didn't even notice it anymore. "After all, all those things used to take place on Earth. Look at the progress we've made: now it takes a whole system to generate the misbehaviour that used to be produced on just one planet.

"Now *that's* progress."

 **OW, HOURS LATER,** Jerry waited with Kat, watching his phone lying face-up on the tabletop beside his drink. Suddenly he perked up.

"Christmas came early. He's moving."

Kat scanned the crowd frantically. Nothing. She couldn't see the telltale olive uniform the guard wore; no one in sight was wearing an officer's cap.

"I don't see him."

"He's here," Jerry answered, still staring down at his phone. "About 50 meters to your left. Just coming out of a doorway in the yellow wall."

Kat squinted in that direction. Still nothing. It had to be right, though; she and Jerry had chosen this spot because they had seen other officers coming from that wall – obviously their offices were located there.

She was feeling panicky. What if the tracking program in Jerry's phone was faulty – she might lose her Slimlines forever! The thought made her shudder.

"Jerry, I'm telling you, I don't –" Kat's mouth snapped shut. She saw him.

He probably thought he was incognito. He had changed from his uniform, was wearing an ugly orange flower print shirt and blue slacks, but Kat recognized him immediately when she spotted his shifty weasel eyes darting back and forth, scanning the crowd, alert for any tourists who might be coming for him.

He walked quickly, head down, but perversely peering upward into the crowd, obviously hoping to look nonchalant while remaining vigilant, but instead looking ridiculous.

Jerry and Kat watched as he scurried past about 15 meters distant, through the crowd, toward the spaceport's main entryway.

Jerry waited until the man was out of sight before he got to his feet. Kat was sweating profusely; her eyes looked pained.

None of her training gave her the patience to play this game – if she had her way, the man would already be lying on the ground, clutching various body parts as they swelled, while Kat basked in the return of her property. Instead she watched Jerry, almost pleading with her eyes.

"Don't worry, baby," said Jerry. "He won't get far. Payday is coming soon."

He dropped a coin on the table and they moved off slowly into the crowd in the direction the man had gone.

I**T WASN'T HARD** to follow him; the spaceport fed right into the largest thoroughfare on the fifth moon. It was a five kilometer stretch of pedestrian chaos. The Spanish authorities had modeled the experience on the downtown corridor of Barcelona's huge pedestrian mall and to their credit, despite the plastic and permafoam construction of the buildings, the same eclectic ambiance pervaded the surroundings. A giddy mix of colours permeated the crowd and the building façades, and the exotic cosmopolitan mix of visitors completed the mélange.

The man Jerry and Kat were following paused every few minutes and pretended to peer intently into random shop windows while covertly scanning the mass of humanity behind him, but in the crush of otherworld tourists he failed to discern his two pursuers.

"I'm running out of patience," whispered Kat during one particularly long stop, as she and Jerry stood motionless in a shadowed doorway, waiting for their prey to resume his journey. "I should have just taken him out the moment he grabbed the glasses."

"Right," whispered back Jerry, "And you'd be having a better time right now shivering naked inside a Placidan interrogation room, I suppose. Or maybe you think they'd have given you guest passes for crippling one of their Customs goons?"

Kat didn't bother responding; their quarry was on the move again.

The streets became noticeably less crowded. The little man made a series of turns into smaller and smaller streets. He looked behind himself often. No one was following him.

Kat and Jerry were forced to stay far back, out of sight. They followed the dot on the tracker, and then suddenly the dot stopped inside a large grey shape on the display.

"Let's go," said Jerry. "He must be home."

They hustled as quickly as they dared through the darkened streets, finally stopping before a nondescript housing block. Checking the display, they entered the building and ran up three flights, turned down a hallway, and stopped outside a door marked "32".

INSIDE, THE LITTLE man stood, sweating, bobbing from foot to foot, twisting his hands, while he watched the large man in front of him holding Kat's Slimlines.

"Why do you think I would want these, Garcia?" asked the man, speaking in rapid Spanish. "I'm only interested in the task we hired you for."

"Yes, yes," replied the little man, "I just thought such a nice machine might be of interest to you, too – it looks very expensive. I'd be happy to let you have it quite cheap…."

The other man looked at him. His expression spoke of great fatigue.

The man's name was Navarro. At least, that was the name he used now. He was a big man, and seemed even more impressive beside the diminutive Customs man. The skin hung on his face in heavy folds, and his hands were swollen with fat. He wore an expensive suit jacket unbuttoned over a clean white shirt. The shirt, though, was mottled with patches of grey as the big man's sweat dampened various segments. His brow furrowed with aggravation as he addressed the little man fidgeting before him.

"Garcia, are you really so stupid you don't realize what this is? You can never use this machine – only its true owner can. And even if it were possible to hack it – which it most assuredly isn't – is this what you take me for? Some cheap crook who buys stolen merchandise?"

"No! No no no no," replied the little man, almost in a frenzy. "No, I would never think such a thing, I just –"

Navarro cut him off with a sharp wave of his hand.

"That's enough. I don't have time for this." He threw the Slimlines at the little man, who fumbled to catch them against his chest before quickly slipping them back into his pants pocket.

"Did the package get on board?"

"Oh, yes sir. Your men – Esteban and Poole, wasn't it? – they came and then left the ship again just before I myself left. They were still in the spaceport moving through the intake lines when I came over here. I thought it would be best to let them leave along with the tourists and other crewmen," he added, almost as an afterthought.

The big man looked at him. He knew the real reason was that Garcia wanted to get here first to beg for his money out of sight of the other men.

"What about the access port?" continued Navarro. "Can we get to it?"

"Yes yes, it's all ready. I set a one-hour delay on the airlock, as you told me. You can use it to get back on the ship until just before departure. No one will see you."

"And you did this yourself?" continued the big man.

"By myself, yes. Only me. I did it all myself." Garcia looked proud.

Navarro was mulling this over, and pondering the best way to kill the little man standing in front of him, when the door behind Garcia erupted in a cascade of splinters and shattered planks.

Along with pieces of the broken door came a human body, bursting in so quickly that neither of the original two occupants of the room had time to do much more than flinch before the intruder had his elbow around Garcia's throat and a hand on the man's sidearm holstered on his right leg.

And then, in one swift motion, he removed his arm from the little man's neck, reached into his pants pocket and grabbed the Slimlines and slipped them into his own pocket.

Then, time stood still.

No one moved.

Jerry liked it that way. He stood, holding the gun, surveying the room, assessing the men. He had been expecting to find only the little man he and Kat had followed, but Jerry was nothing if not versatile. This changed very little.

The big man didn't move so much as a muscle. He sat calmly behind his desk coolly watching Jerry.

He looked over at the shattered doorway behind Jerry's shoulder as Kat tentatively stepped into the room, followed closely by two large men holding two very evil looking pistols.

"Jerry," she said quietly. Jerry still had his back to her.

"Jerry, there's something you need to see," she said.

"**I**NCH AROUND BEHIND me, see if you can reach my hands," whispered Kat.

They were slumped in a back corner of the room, hands and feet bound tightly, all but ignored now as the four other men in the room stood in a tight circle arguing loudly in Spanish.

"What do you think they're saying?" whispered Jerry, microscopically edging towards Kat.

"If I had my Slimlines I could tell you," she replied bitterly. "Why did you stuff them into your damn pocket?"

"If I hadn't that little weasel might still have them. But at least for now it looks like they've got more important things on their minds."

The little Customs man was indeed occupied with far weightier matters. Jerry and Kat's arrival had upset everyone, notwithstanding their immediate capture. The serendipitous arrival of Esteban and Poole had saved the day, but hadn't done anything to calm the fears now plaguing the group of men.

"You were followed!" cursed Navarro, thrusting a meaty finger against Garcia's chest. "Who else? How many others followed you? What else do I need to know?"

"Nothing! No one!" stammered Garcia. "They must have come for the –"

"*Basta!* No more! You're an idiot!" And he reached into his jacket, pulled out a handgun, and fired a white blast into Garcia's chest.

The little man crumpled to the floor accompanied by the acrid smell of charred flesh.

Navarro turned to the other two men standing beside him. Garcia was immediately forgotten, dismissed from their minds as completely as yesterday's weather report.

"We'll need to find out from these two how much they know," he said. "We don't have time to question them here – take them to the ship and hide them somewhere. The Captain doesn't need to know anything about this. Report for duty as usual and work your full shifts. Monitor the ship's communications from your posts in Engineering and contact me immediately if anything out of the ordinary occurs."

He glanced over at Jerry and Kat. Jerry was nonchalantly perched against Kat and his shoulders showed slight movement, almost as though he was working his hands or arms. Navarro abruptly strode over and kicked Jerry in the side of the head, sending him sprawling off to the side, away from Kat. Then he stepped over to Kat and kicked her viciously in the side.

"And keep them separated! They don't see each other again until they meet in Hell."

So saying, he strode out of the room and disappeared down the hallway.

THOSE **W**EDNESDAY **AFTERNOONS** spent practicing Zen had been a good investment, thought Jerry, as he suddenly sat up straight on the bench. He remembered what he needed to know.

A lifetime ago, before Jerry had fled to space, he had enjoyed river rafting. That is, when he could spare the time from his corporate duties. Which was a week every year or so.

And one thing he had learned was that cheap imitation velcro-type hook-and-loop connectors don't hold so well when they get wet, something that not many spacers knew. Water was scarce in space and rarely spilled.

Jerry hopped to the sink, then turned around and hoisted himself up on the edge.

Accidentally overbalancing, he tried to correct himself and immediately fell off. Onto his face. He felt the bone in his nose crunch, and tasted the blood that immediately sprayed out.

God. Could this day get any worse?

Swearing quietly, he got up and carefully perched his butt on the sink's edge. This time, he stayed.

Leaning back, he moved his wrists in front of the sensor and hot water immediately spurted out onto his hands. He let it saturate his wrist straps while he gently twisted and flexed his wrists.

Nothing.

He kept at it, and started to wonder if he could keep it up for much longer; the water was getting progressively hotter.

And then, almost imperceptibly, he felt some movement in the straps.

He redoubled his efforts, flexing and pulling one wrist against the other, twisting in as many directions as he could, virtually willing the straps to loosen.

When they finally came free, they let go so suddenly that Jerry was once again caught off guard and tumbled off the sink.

He would have been able to catch himself this time if his arms hadn't been so numb from their long immobilization. As it was, they merely flopped out to his sides and he plummeted to the deck just as he had before, and this time he bettered the act by hitting his head on the edge of the bench so soundly that it knocked him senseless, and he crumpled onto the deck, blood slowly oozing from a wicked gash in his forehead.

CHAPTER X

KAT'S HEELS WERE both sore before the panel finally cracked. It broke quietly, with a shallow report that was barely audible.

She gave it one more firm whack with her heel and was pleased to see a large wedge of the panel break off and fall into the lit cavity below.

Bright white light from a row of LEDs spilled out of the broken section. Kat twisted her foot around and poked it into the gap. She could feel the broken section moving around, but it took an eternity before she was able to grip it with her toes, and two more tries before she finally lifted it out of the shallow trough, dropping it onto the floor.

She had to lean back then to catch her breath, and was surprised how exhausted she felt. She quickly shook it off, though, and scraped the broken piece of plastic across the floor, first with her foot, then with her ass, until it was within reach of her tied hands.

Her fingers grasped at the broken section and once she had a firm grip she began to saw away at whatever bound her wrists. *Feels like some kind of velcro-type straps – good. Won't take too long.*

Only after she felt the blood dripping did Kat realize that she was making no progress. The only thing she was cutting was the skin off her palms and fingers.

Her mind raced. There had to be a solution – what was she missing?

She turned her head as much as she could and examined the post she was tied to. It was bare and featureless, except for a thick cable running down one side, firmly strapped to the post.

Kat grunted in satisfaction and began to slowly inch her way to her feet. Her ribs screamed in pain, but eventually she was upright, the piece of plastic still in her grasp.

Now for the hard part.

She started scraping the tip of the plastic along the crack between the cable and the post until – *there* – she felt a gap. *Perfect.* She fed one end of the plastic into the crack until it would go no farther, then used the straps on her wrists to jam it as tightly as she could. Soon it was stuck, quite firmly, wedged between the post and the cable.

Undulating like a belly dancer, Kat rubbed her bound wrists carefully up and down along the sharp edge. Her arms couldn't bend to help her, so her body had to provide all the movement. She almost giggled, reflecting how this sight might appear to an observer. She was sure that it would have been appreciated, at least by any male witnesses.

It was a long time before Kat felt the telltale susurration that indicated progress; it was even longer before her labours were fruitful, but eventually Kat found herself with two newly-released arms, and she sank to the floor to wait for her circulation to bring feeling back into them.

THIS TIME, WHEN Jerry's head cleared and his vision stopped spinning, he wasted no time staring at his surroundings.

Cursing the delay, he stretched his arms, flexed his fingers, then immediately bent and plucked at the straps holding his ankles.

Those straps had been secured with a thick band of tape, probably to thwart any attempts his bound hands might have made to pull at the straps. But unbound, his hands made quick work, and in a matter of minutes he was back on his feet, pacing, stretching, and thinking frantically what his next move should be.

Freedom.

He had to get out of this room.

He almost ran around the room, moving in rapid circles, reexamining every detail, pushing against the blank panel of the door, thumping each locker door.

Nothing.

But no, there was *something*.

This was obviously a prep room, a cabin used by spacers to store gear. That would explain the lockers and sink. Perform some particularly nasty maintenance detail, then come in here and wash up and stow your tools.

That means there are power ports in the lockers, at least in *one* locker – a place where power packs can be recharged. And where there is power, there are power problems – failures, overloads, short circuits.

But how to do it? He couldn't get into the locked cabinets. A fly couldn't get in. They were airtight.

No, not airtight, Jerry mused, and then he smiled. *Not even watertight.*

He grabbed the tape from the floor and ran over to the sink. He ran a thick strip of it over the sensor and down into the sink, over the drain. Water started pouring in. In a few minutes, water started pouring out, too, as the sink overflowed and began feeding a puddle on the floor.

It won't be long, thought Jerry. He tried calculating the speed of the puddle's growth, and grimly surmised about thirty minutes would be needed for it to seep into the lockers. *Thirty minutes.*

Ah well, he sighed, maybe in the meantime he could take a bath....

KAT LOOKED AROUND at the various sensors in the room, wondering which she should kill first.

She was scared to randomly vandalize any array, as certain systems – *life support* springs to mind – would not be good to disable.

She could try pulling a connector and then replacing it if the results were unpleasant, but she was concerned that some systems might not reboot without human intervention, and she didn't want to die waiting for her captors to notice the malfunction.

Then on one array she saw a marking on a chip: TEMPCO. She thought back to one of Jerry's endless expositions on the corporate giants of space transportation technology. Tempco was an environmental systems manufacturer producing sensors that controlled the temperature of everything on a ship – air, decking, airless storage bays, conduits, fluids, fuels, everything.

Often there were compounds and modules that needed to stay supercold, while nearby systems might need to operate at normal temperatures. Tempco sensors regulated them all.

What appealed to Kat was the addition of several labels along the side of the array, each indicating a different location.

She found a label marked BRIDGE. She pulled that chip off the board and tossed it to the floor.

She found one marked CREW QUARTERS and another that said OFFICERS MESS. She pulled those, too, then quickly moved over to the door and started smashing the LEDs in the floor strip that illuminated the room. She left one operational, as she couldn't quite bear to wait in complete darkness. It wouldn't be long now, though.

IT TOOK ALMOST the full half hour for the water to reach the bottom of the lockers' doors. And for the last ten minutes Jerry had been getting progressively more impatient. By now he was almost jumping in place, twitching in a frenzied mélange of anxiety and frustration.

As the bottom crack of the lockers was overtaken by the water, Jerry plopped down to his hands and knees to peer as closely as he could at the submerged line. Sure enough, tiny bubbles were escaping from the lockers' interior.

Jerry backed up quickly. If these utility closets were typical, there would be an array of recessed electrical ports inside them, designed to provide recharging for a variety of EV equipment. There was a good chance something might explode, although that wasn't what he was hoping for.

Results came sooner than he'd expected. And quieter.

Without a sound, or even any visible spark, his entire room suddenly went dark. Black as pitch, actually.

Two heartbeats later, the room's emergency systems clicked on.

The water had obviously tripped either an environmental sensor or an electrical safeguard. A long light strip along the ceiling's edge snapped to life, the water pouring from the tap abruptly shut off, and a small, discrete panel beside the pressure door quietly popped open.

Jerry sloshed over to the panel and peered inside.

MANUAL DOOR RELEASE was marked over a white ceramic T-handle. He grabbed the handle, pulled, and twisted.

A soft hiss from the pressure door answered him.

Stealthily, Jerry eased the door open. A small river of water immediately cascaded out and into the corridor.

Jerry hesitated, then threw himself into the corridor outside the room.

No one here, he noted, with a grunt of satisfaction.

The corridor stretched several meters to either side. Jerry could see various machinery poking out into the corridor and huge schematics on the wall. This looked like the Engineering level. Opposite him he could see a ladder in a transit shaft. He ran forward and started climbing.

Jerry exited the shaft at the next level up and ran down a corridor dotted with cabin doors. This looked like a residential level. Just as he was rushing down the corridor he heard a telltale click and pop; he spun and saw a door immediately behind him start to swing inwards. He ran back to the doorway just as a body came into view and threw himself at the emerging occupant, driving the both of them back into the room.

Their two bodies fell to the floor.

Jerry saw he was lying on top of a crewman; this was obviously the man's living quarters.

The man's eyes widened as he saw Jerry's face above him; wild-eyed, face smeared with dry blood around a freshly broken nose and a gashed forehead, Jerry looked like a terrifying madman.

Before the man could grasp what was happening, Jerry twisted him onto his face. He wrapped his arm around the crewman's throat and growled, "I'm not after you – do what I say and you'll walk away unharmed. Or I can kill you now. What's your choice?" He loosened his armlock enough for the man beneath him to gasp, "OK. Whatever you want. OK."

Jerry decided a direct approach was best.

"Where is she? You know who I mean. Where have you got her?"

"OK. Don't squeeze so hard, OK? I can take you to her."

"I don't think so. You tell me where she is – I'll go myself."

"It's not that – you can't get there. She's on a secure level. You can't access it without me."

"You think I'm an idiot?"

"Look buddy," coughed the prone man, his lips mashed against the deck, "I don't give a shit about you or your girl, I just work here. But the sooner you and her are gone, the sooner my life goes back to normal. Your politics means nothing to me."

"Save the bullshit. Tell me how you can get onto a secure level."

"I'm Engineering. There's nowhere I can't go. Comes with the job."

In his previous life Jerry's success had been a consequence of his ability to make good snap decisions. He hoped his instincts were as good in this life.

"OK, let's go," he said.

Dragging the man to his feet, Jerry pulled him over to the small kitchen area in the quarters and grabbed a six-inch chef's knife off the counter. He hoped if he stayed close to the crewman it might be enough to deter any thoughts of resistance.

The two men slipped out into the corridor and jogged down to the nearest transit shaft and slipped into a small elevator. The crewman said "Four" and a wall light blinked green and Jerry felt the momentary sensation of upward movement.

When the door shushed open a few seconds later, Jerry could see before him a distinctly different corridor, dotted with grey panels every few meters along each wall. One was glowing bright red.

"Here you go," said the crewman as they stopped before the lit panel.

Jerry looked dubious.

It seemed too easy. But what choice did he have?

"Open it," he said, and stepped to the side.

KAT THOUGHT SHE was already on edge, but when she heard the voices outside the doorway her heartbeat noticeably pinged higher.

Damn. She'd hoped there would be only one. Well, couldn't be helped.

It hadn't taken long for her to attract attention, no more than 20 minutes or so since she'd disabled the temperature systems.

Showtime. As she thought it, she smiled. That was Jerry's expression. He was becoming a part of her.

Kat's hand nervously gripped a shard of broken plastic, the base wrapped in the straps she had cut off her wrists.

The door began to slide open and Kat tried as best she could to stay behind it. The silhouette of a pistol and then of an extended arm came into view. Kat reached out with her left hand, grabbed the wrist, and pulled the body in as she swung her right arm around in a wide arc, burying the sharp plastic into the throat of the arm's owner. She let it go, leaving it embedded.

Kat was already instinctively leaning back behind the doorway when a beam of blinding white plasma raked past her into the darkened room and seared a hole into the far wall.

Her eyes burned against the bright corridor light but she could still make out another form in the corridor. She pulled the twitching, gurgling body against her, yanked the arm holding the pistol around in front of her, wrapped her fingers around the hand still gripping the weapon and squeezed.

A burst of fire and white light leaped from the gun and

disappeared into the second figure's body. It crumpled to the ground and Kat dropped the convulsing figure and tossed the pistol back into the dark room. There was no point keeping the gun, since pulse weapons are keyed to the real owner's biosignal.

Ignoring the blood and bodies, Kat leaped into the corridor and ran without bothering to choose a direction. Her eyes were still blinded by the corridor light and she didn't have the luxury of waiting until they adjusted to look at corridor markings.

Her bare feet slipped on the decking and she skidded against a bulkhead. *What the …?* A pool of water covered the floor, with even more still streaming out of an open doorway. She looked inside the room. Empty, except for a mini lake sloshing around on the other side of the open pressure door.

I've got to get as far away from here as I can, she thought. *There's some weird shit happening here.*

She had to find Jerry. *Damn! I wish I had my glasses!*

Kat came to a side corridor. Without hesitation she turned down it. She immediately felt less exposed than she had in the main corridor, but not by much, considering how she was dressed.

As her vision recovered, wall markings came into focus.

Looks like Engineering. That explains the room I was locked in.

The corridor widened into a small holding area and Kat saw benches and rows of suits hung above them. *No EV suits*, she noted ruefully, but lots of radiation suits. *Typical for engineering.* Most work would be performed in pressurized areas, but around dangerous equipment. She sized up the suits and picked what looked to be the smallest one. Slipping into it, she checked the nameplate on the chest. *J Chen.*

Shit. With her bright red hair no way she looked like a *J Chen*.

Oh well, if it comes to that I'm toast anyway. It's still better than scampering around in my underwear.

Once she was suited-up she made a point to calm herself and slow her breathing. She knew what to do now.

Five meters down the corridor Kat found a large schematic on the wall. There were blinking red lights scattered around the display. Kat smiled. *Looks like my handiwork*, she chuckled.

She looked up at the ID markings on the wall above her, then back to the schematic. It took a few seconds before she found her position and only a few more before she decided where she needed to go.

Minutes later, she stepped out of a side utility corridor into a wide open area where a half dozen techs in rad suits similar to hers bustled around in a frenzy, busily poking at consoles and workstations. No one noticed her; the noisy chaos of the group spoke of confusion and barely-suppressed panic.

Kat quick-walked over to a discrete workstation, turned her back to the room and bent over the console, trying her best to become invisible. She listened as intently as she could to the jumble of voices around her, trying to pick out a coherent conversation.

"Down to nine degrees in CQ," called out a tense voice nearby. "And up to almost fifty-seven on the bridge. Soon they'll be able to fry eggs on their consoles if this keeps up."

"What in hell is taking Esteban and Poole so damn long to report?" replied a different voice, this one reeking of frustration, verging on the edge of screaming. "At the speed they raced out of here? Those bums never moved that fast in their lives, and now they disappear? What shit are they pulling now?"

Are those the two I took out? Kat wondered. None of the workers around her wore sidearms, she noted, discreetly peering out of the corners of her eyes. Maybe only a few crewmen were involved in the monkey business. She made a mental note not to kill anyone else; despite the danger she was in, Kat wanted to avoid harming an innocent crewman. The only problem would be figuring out who the bad guys were.

"Someone go find those assholes," continued the second voice.

"It's gotten so hot on the bridge they're going to evacuate."

"– And take sidearms from the weapons locker! No telling what bullshit we're involved in now."

Better and better, thought Kat. If they hadn't already, they'd have to drop out of lightspeed if they were evacuating the bridge. That would make escape possible – you couldn't exit a ship traveling at lightspeed.

Even without her Slimlines Kat knew her way around a computer. In less than a minute she had found a schematic showing the shuttle bay. She tapped a few spots on the display and was pleased to see corresponding green lights illuminate on the screen. Shuttle bay controls were now unlocked and accessible from inside the bay.

She had no intention of leaving Jerry behind; a shuttle was simply the best place to hide. If she were lucky, she'd be able to link into the main ship's computer from there. So far she saw no indications on this system where he might be held, but knowing Jerry something was bound to pop up.

She tapped the display and pulled up a schematic for the crew recreation area, then turned and walked away from the display as quickly as she dared, back in the direction from which she'd come. Anyone who checked her workstation might be misled into thinking that's where she was headed. Every little bit helped.

Kat turned back into the transitway from which she'd come. She headed down the corridor and ran smack dab into an engineer emerging from a cross corridor.

"Hey!" blurted the surprised man.

"Hey yourself," replied Kat, as she grabbed the man by the throat, swung his head as hard as she could into the bulkhead wall, and watched him crumple at her feet. She bent down and checked him quickly. Still breathing. OK then.

Without looking back, she continued on her path towards the shuttle bay.

AS JERRY'S CAPTIVE crewman pressed the red panel it recognized the biometric signature and the cabin door swung inwards.

Jerry pushed the man into the room and stood back. He knew Kat; if she was still alive it would be very dangerous for anyone entering this room. He waited for her to "greet" her visitor.

Nothing.

Tentatively, he peered into the room. The crewman was standing just inside the doorway. A female figure sat meekly on a bed against the far wall.

It was not Kat.

"What are you pulling?" screamed Jerry, slamming the crewman forward. "I told you not to –"

"Are you nuts?" hollered the crewman. "You wanted me to take you to her, you crazy asshole! Here's your precious princess! We're done! Take her and get the hell away from me!"

Jerry blinked. The crewman sounded too frustrated to be lying.

"Princess"?

Oh no.

CHAPTER XVI

NAVARRO PACED in his cabin.

This was not an insignificant activity.

A man of his size believed in economy of movement, and to pace indicated extreme internal distress.

He muttered a string of curses interspersed with the late Garcia's name. Months of planning. *Months!* And now everything was crumbling before his very eyes.

He'd known the little Customs man was the weak link in the chain, but essential nonetheless. It had been simply impossible to find another way to smuggle the princess onboard. Garcia had been a choice of last resort. The other Customs men had all been too proud or too patriotic to respond to his first tentative feelers. Only a true worm like Garcia had shown the essential combination of greed and a lack of loyalty to his homeworld.

The fools! As if Navarro gave a rat's ass about Domingan politics. The princess would fetch a ransom big enough to buy a nation – what did he care about the petty separatist squabbles that infested this system like so many fleas on a dog.

He had to admit, though, the political ramifications had benefited him well. Captain Asunción was as uninterested in the ransom as Navarro was in the politics. That suited them both.

As soon as they'd entered lightspeed, Asunción had announced to the crew that they had all embarked on a glorious mission to liberate their homeworld.

When he bragged about their royal prisoner and how her capture would glorify their noble cause, the crew reacted less than enthusiastically, thought Navarro.

He'd been in the Officers Mess when the Captain's announcement played throughout the ship. There were no happy smiles.

These were working men, professional spacers putting in their three-to-five-year tours mining ore on Placidan asteroids – politics was not in their range of interests. Almost all came from other parts of the galaxy, and some of them didn't even speak Spanish.

But no crewman contradicted the Captain. Navarro could tell they didn't like it, but they'd keep taking orders as long as they continued to get paid.

But now.

Now there was trouble.

Ten minutes earlier Navarro had got a message from Esteban. Environmental controls had suddenly crashed in several sectors.

Navarro was beside himself. Were they being betrayed from within? Esteban had told him it looked like the systems might be failing in one of the rooms where they'd hidden the prisoners – where the girl was, actually.

He'd gone to check, taking Poole with him.

Navarro sighed. Esteban was good, but too sure of himself. He had the typical male bravado in spades, and Navarro doubted that Esteban really believed a girl could be dangerous.

He'd better follow up. He didn't want this situation getting out of hand.

And besides, his cabin was getting uncomfortably cold. He could almost see his breath.

Navarro squeezed through his cabin doorway and lumbered off towards the elevator. Esteban had given him the prisoners' locations – they were on Engineering.

CHAPTER XVII

THE ROOM SWAM before Jerry's eyes. He couldn't think this fast.

"Are there any other prisoners on this ship?" he asked the crewman.

"*Other* prisoners? What kind of people do you think we are? You think we do this all the time?"

Jerry stopped listening while the crewman continued ranting. This was pointless, he decided. He needed to stop and regroup. He couldn't do Kat any good if he got killed or recaptured.

One thing, though. He looked up at the girl, still sitting on the bed.

"You. Come." He didn't know her language but his meaning was clear.

Without a word, she rose from the bed and walked over to him. Jerry grabbed her wrist and turned to the crewman.

"OK. Your part's almost done," he lied. "Get me to a shuttle and we're out of your hair."

No one said anything else. The crewman angrily pushed past Jerry and jogged to the elevator. Jerry and the princess followed on his heels.

THE ELEVATOR DOOR hissed open and Navarro strode purposefully into the corridor. Turning at an intersection, he saw before him, ten feet away, the crumpled forms of his two associates lying on the decking.

One lay face down in an enormous pool of blood, the other sat slumped over, displaying only a charred, freshly-cauterized hole in his back.

This was bad.

He turned back towards the elevator just as two rad-suited men sporting sidearms emerged from a side access door.

The men's gaze flashed at Navarro, then at the figures on the deck, then back to the big man, now standing stock still, hands at his sides, watching them both.

Both men raised their weapons. They looked very nervous.

"Hold it right there, sir," barked one of them, but his voice betrayed a nervous confusion.

Navarro stayed motionless. He knew what frightened civilians could do with sidearms, and he had no intention of provoking any panicked responses.

The men took a step forward, and one of them suddenly flipped backwards into the air as his feet slipped on a water-covered area of decking. Falling, he inadvertently squeezed the trigger on his gun, and a long white blast of light streamed out and painted a jagged black line on the bulkhead.

His companion, jittery to begin with, jerked back and pressed the trigger on his own gun, still leveled perfectly at Navarro's chest.

As he felt his insides being flash-broiled, Navarro had a second to reflect how easily even the best-laid plans can go tragically wrong when you hire cheap labour.

CHAPTER XIX

THE ELEVATOR STOPPED on the Engineering level and the trio pushed out into the corridor.

Jerry had chosen to take the elevator nearest the shuttle bay. There would be too much activity on the Engineering level to make it through safely.

They emerged at a deserted end of a long companionway.

"Twenty meters ahead," said the crewman. "And do me a favour."

"Yeah?"

"Don't come back. I never see you again, it's too soon."

"You got it," lied Jerry again.

Doesn't this guy realise I need his biosignature to activate the shuttle? Oh well, that's news I don't have to break to him until we get there.

Jerry's mind was racing.

As he saw it, his best hope for getting Kat back alive lay in developing some leverage. He didn't like it, but the best leverage he could come up with was the princess at his side. He couldn't imagine actually handing the girl back to the goons who'd kidnapped her, but that was a problem he'd have to confront later.

For now, he needed to get to a place of safety, and that meant off this ship.

As they hustled down the corridor they passed two side transitways where Jerry saw rad suited workers running around. Farther down their own passageway Jerry saw a figure in a rad suit turn off to the side and disappear, and ten meters farther down, at the end, an airlock. The shuttles were on the other side.

They barreled down the corridor, moving so intently that Jerry almost didn't realize there was someone behind him. Almost.

He didn't hear anything, he *felt* the presence. Someone had slipped out of a side transitway after they'd passed.

Right hand in his pocket, his fingers gripped the knife tightly; his pace changed ever so slightly and he readied himself to shift his weight and spin around.

"For God's sake, Jerry," came a voice, "You're out of my sight for ten minutes and you pick up another woman?"

WATCHING THE CREWMAN pull open the airlock door, Kat raked her eyes disapprovingly over Jerry.

"Leaving me, were you? You and your pretty captive speeding off into inky space without a thought for my wellbeing?"

Jerry laughed softly.

"And you, Kat? Where were you going? Just happened to be sightseeing beside the shuttle bay?"

Kat returned the laugh. "Only looking for you, babe. I figured the exit was where you'd be."

The crewman looked over at them in disbelief.

"Just how many of you are on this ship, anyway?" he asked.

They stepped into the shuttle bay. A dozen craft were lined up. Jerry turned to the crewman.

"Look," he said. "You seem like a straight-up guy. Why don't you find an honest ship to work on? You can do better than this.

"Thanks for your help. We'll be gone before you can do anything to stop us –" Jerry's eyes flickered over to Kat and the princess as they jogged to the closest shuttle. He could see Kat's lips moving; her Slimlines were already powering up the shuttle systems. If the alarm stayed off for sixty more seconds they'd be away.

Regretting it even before he spoke, Jerry said to the crewman, "—unless you want to come with us. You might do well to vamoose now."

The crewman smiled, then turned back to the airlock.

"No thanks," he said, stopping to look at Jerry's bruised and bloodied face. "I don't think I want to end up looking like you."

KAT WAS FAST, thought Jerry. He had to scramble to get on board before the shuttle started to move, and the shuttle bay doors were only about a third open when their craft burst out between them.

The princess was already on the comms talking to her frantic father. She motioned to Kat, who linked-in to the call and synched her Slimlines with the ship's nav system and downloaded the Palace coordinates.

The princess looked up at Jerry with tears in her eyes. Jerry had a feeling he and Kat were going to be treated *very* well at the Palace.

They were initiating lightspeed when Jerry asked, "Any sign of pursuit or attack from the mothership?"

Kat laughed sharply. "I don't think that's likely, Jerry. See this readout?"

Jerry squinted up at a number on a display. "Eighty-eight Celsius? What is that – about 200 degrees Fahrenheit? Yeah? So?"

"At that temperature, I think the bridge personnel are too busy imitating weenies on a grill to bother with little old us," replied Kat with a smirk.

Weenies on a grill, thought Jerry. He tried to recall when he'd said that to Kat. He'd have to be careful what he said in the future – she obviously remembered everything he said.

He couldn't remember ever feeling happier.

pleasure cruise

CURSING SILENTLY, KAT scratched frantically for a finger-hold on the slick ceramic skin of the ship. But the surface was flawlessly smooth, without even so much as a seam or rivet point.

She was sliding faster now; she had no tools left to slow her velocity in the frictionless void of space. The hull passed by so quickly beneath her desperate grasp it was a blur.

To make matters worse, the farther she slid the more steeply the hull declined as the stern gently curved downwards. In a minute she wouldn't just be skidding over the smooth surface, she would actually leave it and drift off into space. She would already have floated off if it weren't for the ship's weak gravity that still gently pulled her.

But even now she could feel her every frantic scratch pushing her off just a little bit more.

The stern of the ship rushed toward her at breakneck speed. It was now a matter of mere seconds.

When the moment did come she almost couldn't tell. She was no longer in contact with the hull, and one second she was watching it zip by her plummeting form, and the next she had passed it and dropped off helplessly into the void.

She tilted her head back and saw the underbelly of the huge starship above her. As she slowly started to rotate end over end, she watched the ship move lower in her vision while her body did a slow-motion backflip in the darkness. Just as the last image of the ship disappeared behind her feet she heard the chime in her helmet as her suit announced, "All oxygen has been expended. System shutting down."

And her helmet – along with the rest of her suit – went dark.

GOTTA HAND IT to you, Kitty-kat," mused Jerry, "This is one fine-ass ship you picked out for us."

Kat smiled softly at his comment. Jerry usually only called her that when he was feeling frisky, and she was happy to see him so at ease.

Her – correction: *their* – last big payday had been enough to set them up comfortably for years to come, but Jerry had pushed for them to blow a big part of it on a new ship. He was perceptive enough to know that Kat wouldn't be happy laying on a beach somewhere for more than a few weeks, at most, before she got to yearning for life on the road once again.

He had let Kat pick out the ship but he'd made it clear that comfort was paramount. They'd each need plenty of personal space; both he and Kat had been living solitary lives before they met and it was essential to have a private place to withdraw to from time to time.

The ship they'd chosen fit the bill perfectly.

In addition to a spacious lounge, a well-appointed kitchen and a decadent master bedroom, there was a private room for Jerry (which he insisted on referring to as his "office"), and another for Kat.

In no time at all Jerry's office became cluttered with all the knickknacks, manuals, tools and doodads that had no proper place anywhere else in the ship.

Kat's room, though, was so spare as to be almost barren, with little besides a foam Yoga mat on the floor and two tapestries on the wall from the Sillestrian Monastery on Tamara Prime.

But to both Jerry's and Kat's surprise, neither room was very often occupied. The simple fact was, they loved each other's company so much they couldn't bear to be apart.

So they each hung out on the bridge most of their waking hours, Kat watching vids on her Slimlines and Jerry tinkering with the ship and tweaking its systems.

They were headed nowhere in particular, which was perfect Retriever behaviour, because no one knew where in the universe the next great Discovery would be found. Aimless wandering was every bit as valid as carefully plotted journeys laid out months in advance. Luck was the lion's share of every Retriever's fortune.

Consequently, they were jumping randomly across a set of star systems in the Rostov Constellation when they came across the casino cruise ship *Buona Fortuna* docked at the Yusupov Starbase while taking on supplies.

The *Fortuna* was a sight to behold, appearing from a distance like a big fat hot dog wiener wrapped in a shorter, fatter transparent bun.

In actuality, the "bun" part was a clear outer dome that wrapped most of each side of the ship so the tourists could stroll along the "outside" of many of the 90 decks and recline in chaise longues while they gazed at the stars passing by.

"Inside" the ship, casinos, restaurants, shopping malls and a multitude of artificial lakes, beaches and swimming pools provided the passengers with a smorgasbord of entertainments.

It was too serendipitous an encounter to pass up. With little more than a quick nod of agreement between them, Jerry hailed the ship and booked a cabin for a week-long stay.

They docked on the underside of the cruiser where huge clamps and access tubes snaked out to grip their ship and connect them to a boarding port.

"I don't have anything to wear!" wailed Kat, looking despairingly at her near-empty closet.

"Baby, I guarantee you there will be clothing stores on this thing that could dress you for the rest of your life," replied Jerry.

"I might even find something for myself," he added.

Kat watched him as he tossed two t-shirts and a clean set of socks and underwear into a small duffel bag before zipping it closed.

"You're kidding, right?" she asked, nodding at his bag.

"Nope. This is how a real *man* packs."

Seeing her dumbstruck expression verging on the edge of horror, he quickly added, "Until I've had a chance to shop as well. After lunch, that is…."

GÜNTER **K**LUM leaned back from the monitor and rubbed his eyes. Spending the greater part of his days sitting in a dimly-lit room buried in the bowels of the ship was hardly what he had expected when he'd signed on as Security Supervisor.

Günter wasn't a big man, standing only 5'10", but he was solid, mostly muscle and very little fat. When he wasn't on duty he could usually be found in the staff gym, lifting weights, boxing, running, doing whatever he could to maintain his athletic physique.

His hair was cut short, in a military style. He had no facial hair nor any tattoos. He carefully maintained his appearance, dressing in tailored suits that were stylish but not ostentatious. He wore no jewelry, except for a chrome diving watch that kept perfect time.

Günter considered himself a serious professional. He kept to himself, focused on his duties, was never late to arrive on shift and never early to leave.

Despite all this, he didn't feel he was properly appreciated by Management. His current assignment could be adequately performed by a trained monkey, in his opinion. The Chief of Security, a pustulent fat blob of a man who was too lazy to ever actually leave his office, had condescended to explain that he was assigning Günter to Screening and Tracking as a means of acquainting him with the ship's layout and various activities.

But after five months of watching a monitor Günter began wondering if his title was more of a euphemism than an actual mark of authority. Most of the other schmucks stuck in the monitoring center also sported titles like 'supervisor', 'coordinator', and 'director'. In fact, directly across from him sat the Director of Verification, a tired woman pushing fifty who stared unblinkingly at her monitor with even less enthusiasm than Günter had for his own.

He glanced up at her over his monitor screen. It seemed to him that she had developed a slight twitch in her left eye. In fact, her gaze looked unfocused, and he wondered if she was even paying attention to the image in front of her at all. She looked a thousand miles away. *Probably dreaming about laying on a beach under a warm sun,* he thought.

Günter lowered his eyes back to the screen and resumed watching the stream of humanity flowing by. Above each person's head floated a coloured symbol representing their threat assessment as calculated by the entry screening software. Image recognition would forever pair the people with their symbols wherever they went on the ship. It made a security man's life just a little bit easier.

Orange triangles meant contraband had been detected in their luggage or on their person. Red stars were for those found with weapons. Green dollar signs were reserved for VIPs, especially wealthy guests and those carrying large amounts of cash. Blue squares were for non-gamblers, and pink circles were for underage passengers. A bright yellow question mark floated above first-time guests who were otherwise without distinction.

There were a host of variations on these codes but Günter concentrated only on the red stars.

He tapped the screen and froze the display on one individual who seemed especially shady. The person's eyes were darting back and forth as he walked, and he sported not just a red star but an orange triangle and a green dollar sign, as well. He looked like a little Christmas ornament as he slithered through the crowd heading up the gangway into reception.

Günter tapped the screen again and a list appeared on the right, detailing the man's assessment.

Tried to board with cigarettes, alcohol, two wrist darts, one ceramic ankle knife, and fifty thousand credits in cash notes. Relieved of all of the above except the cash notes. (The casino would perform that last task in no time, thought Günter.)

Tobacco products and alcohol were both sold throughout the ship. You could buy as much as you want on board and leave with it, but nothing comes in except through ship's stores; anything you tried to board with was confiscated. As for weapons, they were confiscated too and you were given a warning; the next attempt would get you permanently barred.

He marked the man as a person of interest. His system would now keep him apprised of the man's movements. Günter unfroze his display and the crowd surged back to life.

It wasn't until almost the end of his shift that he spotted something that caught his attention again.

It wasn't the symbol above their heads (yellow question mark) but rather the shapely form of the woman that caught his eye. Günter was a man like any other, and his attention was invariably drawn to the more attractive members of the opposite sex.

He watched her carefully as she undulated across his display, and he glanced enviously at her companion, whose arm she wrapped in her own as they walked.

He saw the man's face, blinked, froze his display, then zoomed in. He let out a little grunt of recognition as the man's features filled the screen. Yep. That was him alright.

Günter tapped the screen and marked the couple in his system.

JERRY AND KAT were like two teenagers on their first trip away from home. They oohed and aahed at the goods on display in the shop windows, examined every restaurant menu, and browsed through every souvenir shop they came across. At the first Tobacconist they saw Jerry was quick to buy an actual honest-to-goodness Cuban cigar. From Earth, no less.

"I used to smoke these Cohibas nonstop in my first life, when I was a Titan of Industry," he told Kat, clamping his teeth around the fat stogie in self-satisfaction.

"Hey, feel free to wander down Memory Lane all you want, bub, but if you light that thing up anywhere near me be prepared for a sudden shower," she replied, eyeing the cigar with distaste.

"No worries there, hon. I don't need to smoke 'em anymore, but it sure is a good feeling to chomp on one from time to time, even if it's unlit."

Kat had her own indulgences, pressing her nose against the glass of every exotic electronics shop along the pedestrian thoroughfare.

"How can this ship maintain all these shops?" she wondered, gazing down the seemingly endless vista. "I can't even see the end of this promenade."

"As I understand it," said Jerry, "There are well over two hundred thousand passengers on board at any time, and I wouldn't want to even speculate how many staff to add to that. This is a *huge* operation."

But he was talking to himself. Kat had skipped away to delightedly ogle a pair of diamond earbuds that she thought would make just the *perfect* accessory to her Slimlines....

CHAPTER IV

GÜNTER KEPT AN eye on the shifty little man for the next three days. His behaviour was not what Günter had been expecting.

The Weasel (as Günter had nicknamed him) didn't seem to be interested in drinking or gambling or in doing any of the other things that drew the tourists to the ship, with one exception. The man appeared to be a fan of one particular live theater performance that the ship produced.

He attended every matinee and evening performance in one specific theater, seeing the same show as many as three times in a day. He remained long after the performances were over, apparently sticking around to hang out with the stage crew. Normally, Günter would just have pegged him as a theater groupie, a wannabe actor getting his kicks hanging out behind the scenes. But on the third day he noticed him talking with a certain stage hand and Günter quickly retrieved and played back the other surveillance vids and noticed that the Weasel always spoke with the same guy and seemed to be focused only on him.

The evening of the fourth day Günter was just settling down to run the recordings of the Weasel's recent movements when all the surveillance monitors suddenly started strobing bright red. He tapped a key and brought up a live view of the problem area.

Three Security men were facing down a lone individual, who occasionally leaned out of an alcove to spray them with ball bearings from a handheld launcher. One additional guard was laying prone on the decking, a nasty red stain slowly darkening the tile beneath him.

The assailant was Günter's Weasel.

Shit! mouthed Günter silently, springing up from his chair and launching himself through the doorway and off down the corridor towards the conflict zone.

This was going to come back and bite him – it would soon become clear that he'd tagged the guy in his system and should have been on top of this situation. Management would be looking for scapegoats and his name would be at the top of the list.

Five months of thankless toil down the drain. This little debacle would probably condemn him to his surveillance monitor forever if he weren't fired outright.

Günter barreled down the corridor at top speed, yelling at tourists as he bore down on them, dodging those too old or too clueless to move aside in time.

He leapt into the elevator bay and right into one that was just about to close.

"Everybody out! NOW!" he yelled at the startled passengers.

He bodily shoved out two slowpokes before he rapidly punched in an emergency code and held on as the elevator doors swished shut and the machine shot up sixty-five decks to where the altercation was taking place.

When the elevator came to a stop and the doors slid open, Günter spun and dropped to the deck as a volley of pellets whizzed past his face and slammed into the bulkhead to his right.

The three Security men were still cowering at the end of a cross corridor just in front of him while the Weasel leaned out and waved his weapon.

Günter chanced a peek out of the elevator down towards the shooter, just in time to see two more Security men burst from a passageway directly behind the Weasel. They stopped dead in their tracks, obviously surprised to find themselves in such a vulnerable position, without any barrier between them and the gunman.

But rather than shoot at them, the little man suddenly turned on his heels and disappeared down the side corridor where he'd been cowering.

Günter quickly replayed in his mind the floor plan of this particular section. One thing his boss had gotten right: the last few months staring into security monitors certainly had taught Günter the layout of the ship.

He realized immediately that there was virtually no place for the Weasel to run to down that corridor – it ended in a long, wide balcony that overlooked the starboard atrium, sixty decks high, affording a breathtaking view of the stars beyond the huge viewing dome that enclosed most of the starboard side of the ship.

He bolted from the elevator down towards the corridor where the little man had disappeared. The two newly arrived Security men were only steps ahead of him as he turned the corner and spotted the man pressed up against the balcony railing, trapped.

The word "No!" froze on his lips as he saw, in a lightning flash, one of the Security men raise up a stun gun, point it at the little man, and fire.

The rest of the scene played out in what seemed to Günter like a very predictable slow-motion sequence: the Security man fired, the Weasel twitched convulsively, recoiling from the shock, stumbled, and flipped backwards over the balcony railing.

The last sight Günter had of him was the soles of his shoes as he dropped below the balcony's edge and into the void.

KAT AND JERRY were savouring the ship's pseudo-Italian atmosphere, delighted to play the part of awestruck tourists. They were presently enjoying after-dinner drinks at a quaint little sidewalk café situated in an impressive reproduction of the plaza in front of Rome's Pantheon.

Above them, a pale blue "sky" slowly darkened in the simulated dusk. About a dozen pigeons fluttered around, landing occasionally to peck at bits of bread tossed into the street by fellow diners.

"They really did a good job with this place," said Jerry, chomping on his cigar and cradling a wine glass. "I've been to this plaza. If I squint my eyes I'd swear I was there again right now."

"I've been to Rome, too," answered Kat, "And I don't remember the Trevi fountain being anywhere near the Pantheon."

Jerry looked off to his left. Sure enough, at the end of the block the street widened out again and the Trevi fountain plaza glittered away in the distance.

"Well, I suppose there's only so much room here. Probably around the other corner we can find the Coliseum."

Kat giggled and sipped her wine. "The food's good, too. So far, I think I might give this place five stars."

Just at that moment the strangest crescendo of a wail gradually filled the air and then was abruptly cut off as a man's body suddenly popped into view, bursting through the fake sky to plunge directly into the middle of the plaza, smashing straight down into the Pantheon fountain and drenching several bystanders in a huge splash of water.

No one screamed. There were perhaps one or two shocked gasps, but for the most part, everyone just stopped and stared in stunned surprise. A pit-pat of water drops dripping from various surfaces punctuated the scene. The man in the fountain didn't move at all.

"*Definitely* five stars," said Kat quietly, picking up her glass and taking another sip.

GÜNTER WAS DESPONDENT.

The proverbial shit had indeed impacted squarely against his own personal fan. His boss screamed at him so extensively and with such vigour that Günter was afraid the man would actually burn off a calorie.

Günter was charged with gross incompetence, reprimanded for failure to recognize the egregiously suspicious behaviour that the Weasel had been engaging in, and tasked with reconstructing a detailed minute-by-minute itinerary of every single action the Weasel had taken when not in his cabin.

If there were any silver lining to the coal-black cloud of misery that encased Günter, it was that the Weasel, miraculously, had not quite died. The thin plaster "sky" above the Pantheon plaza had broken his fall just enough to allow him to impact the water in the fountain at slightly less than a fully lethal speed. His spine was shattered, both arms and legs broken in multiple locations, he'd suffered a concussion and had two collapsed lungs, but he was still alive.

The doctors had worked a miracle with the little man. His regenerated lungs were just barely able to maintain his breathing with the assistance of a rich oxygen mixture pumped into his nose. Unfortunately, his spine was a total loss and the bleeding in his brain continued unabated, threatening to crush his brain against his skull.

But he was alive.

Günter was sitting morosely beside the Weasel's bed contemplating the train wreck his career had become when the little man regained consciousness and croaked a word.

"Water."

Günter jumped so hard he almost lost his balance on his chair. He looked at the little man in shock and immediately reached out to the nurse call button.

"No."

The word was a soft croak, but enough to stop Günter halfway through his motion. Instead, he turned and reached over to a tray and picked up a small paper cup and lowered it to the man's lips, letting a few drops dribble into his mouth. The man's tongue barely flicked at his cracked lips, but his face slightly relaxed and he let out a long sigh.

"I want… to make… a deal," came the tortured whisper from the wrecked form in the bed.

"A deal? You're talking to the wrong guy, buddy. I just work here."

The little man let the slightest hint of a smile twist one of his lips. "I don't think so." – cough – "I think you can… help me out, and I can" – cough – "help you."

Günter paused for a minute, thinking.

What did he have to lose here? He certainly owed no allegiance to the ship. They'd made it clear he would be hung out to dry over this fiasco. Two Staff dead, and the perp critically injured. Forget about loyalty: there were lawsuits coming and the ship wanted his head.

Günter leaned over the Weasel's bed and whispered, "Tell me how I can help you."

JERRY TAPPED THE green felt in front of him and the dealer laid another card down on the king and the two.

"Too many," said the dealer, sweeping away his cards and chips.

Jerry sighed and watched the rest of the hands play out.

This wasn't as much fun without Kat beside him. He kept unconsciously turning to the side to make a comment, and then abruptly shutting his mouth when he realized she wasn't there.

Jerry and Kat had been on board five days and were still exploring the huge vessel. They spent their days laying on the beach soaking up the "sun" and whiled away their evenings in the nightclubs and cabarets. Tonight they thought they'd try the casino.

Of course Kat's Slimlines weren't allowed in the casino. The security gate had softly chimed as they'd approached and a very polite gentleman had explained that she would have to leave them in a convenience locker while she was on the casino floor. Naturally, that wasn't an option for her.

So she'd given Jerry a quick peck on the mouth, wished him good luck, then swept off to relax in the lounge with a drink and a view of the nebula off their starboard beam.

But Jerry wasn't enjoying the casino as much as he'd expected. Without Kat to banter with he felt antsy, and after only twenty minutes he was already contemplating wandering off to find her.

Just then, he felt a soft touch on his shoulder.

"Jerome," said a deep voice behind his left ear. He turned and looked into a pair of steely blue eyes in a serious face. He noticed peripherally the discreet security emblem pinned on a lapel.

"It's me," said the face. "Günter. Günter Klum. Remember? From Agrus 9 – the barley harvest?"

"Günter!" A flash of recognition lit Jerry's face, and a broad smile filled his face as he turned to grip Günter's hand in a hearty handshake. "I'd never have recognized you! What are you doing in that monkey suit? That's a pretty big change from farm overalls!"

"Isn't it, though? And I could say the same about you.

"Say," continued Günter, "Can I steal you away from the table for a few minutes so we can catch up? How about you let me buy you a drink – there's a quiet lounge just one deck away."

"That's a great idea, Gun. I was just about to leave anyways," said Jerry, sweeping up his remaining chips. "But let's stop to collect my girl from the lounge – I'd love to introduce you."

"And I'd love to meet her. But I think that'll have to wait for later. This conversation I need to have with you alone."

JERRY CALLED KAT and explained cryptically that he was "in conference" on "a Security matter" and told her she could head back to their cabin without him; he'd come up when his meeting was over. He cut off her inevitable questions and followed Günter into the lounge.

After a few minutes of small talk Günter turned to Jerry and said, "Jerome, a certain situation has arisen here on the ship that I could really use some help with. And coming across you at just this time seems too fortuitous to pass up. Would you be willing to give me a hand with a little detective work?"

"Detective work?" replied Jerry with a quizzical little smile. "Are you sure you don't have me confused with someone else? I really work better with my hands."

"Don't kid me, Jerome. You're not fooling anyone with that 'aw shucks' act. You've got one of the sharpest minds I know and this job requires a truly deductive intellect – as well as a certain amount of... ah, *discretion*...."

"So it's illegal."

"No! Well, not *per se*. But I do want to keep it under the radar. There are several other parties who might become interested if the facts get out.

"And there's a very large payday if we're successful.

"*Very* large."

"You've got my attention, Gun. Expound away."

"OK, let's start at the beginning – have you ever heard of Goldenroot? No? Well, very few people have. It's a delicate flower that has only ever been found in one place, on a tiny island on the water planet of Noor.

"The lucky thing was, there's so little land on the planet, and consequently so few plants and insects, the herbologists and entomologists had a field day collecting and cataloguing samples. They thought they might actually be able to catalogue every living non-aquatic entity on a planet for the first time ever. There couldn't have been more than one or two thousand unique life forms, so they went at it with gusto.

"Unfortunately for the Goldenroot plant, almost immediately after it was collected it was discovered to possess an incredible compound that can make any organic form increase in size, a bit like a growth enhancer. The first researcher to handle the plant without gloves quickly found his fingers increasing in size like little sausages. Further testing shows the plant will grow any appendage on the human body to larger size, usually increasing by 20 to 30% whatever it is topically applied to.

"*Permanently increasing in size*," repeated Günter meaningfully. "With no side effects."

Günter paused for a moment to let this information become clear to Jerry.

"OK," said Jerry, "So if you want larger… fingers…."

"That's right," replied Günter. "Fingers. Because every guy wants to have larger *fingers*."

"Riiiiiight…" continued Jerry. "*Any* appendage? 20 to 30% larger?"

"Now you understand," said Günter. "But here's the punch line: the Goldenroot plant is a finicky little thing. It won't grow in the lab, it won't grow from culture, it has no seed and can't be transplanted. The only place where it can grow is in its native environment, spontaneously producing new shoots from an existing plant.

"It grows extremely slowly and, to make matters worse, there are probably only about a dozen flowers left alive that haven't been collected. And those dozen are now cordoned off in one of the tightest quarantine zones you can imagine. The Interstellar Consortium doesn't want to wipe this little treasure from the Universe until they figure out how to synthesize or reproduce it."

"So how does this involve us?"

"It involves us precisely because of its insane scarcity. There exist only two small vials of Goldenroot extract that were processed in the lab before the axe came down.

"Naturally, and I'm sure this doesn't shock you, some slimeball stole these vials and sold them to a certain individual who is ridiculously wealthy and has everything one could want in life except – one must assume – one particular attribute. This individual was willing to pay an astronomical sum to achieve what billions of similarly-endowed men can only dream about.

"And then someone stole it again.

"And that person then boarded this very ship."

Günter stopped talking and let the thought hang in the air. His eyes scanned the room, as though he were checking for eavesdroppers on their conversation.

"Is that all?" said Jerry. "Don't tell me – you said 'boarded', so I'm assuming this person vamoosed and now you want to track him down. You don't need a detective for that. You should hardly break a sweat finding this clown. No one can go anywhere these days without leaving a dozen digital trails behind."

"Actually, Jerry, I already know where he is. And in point of fact, he is still on board this ship.

"As you said, no one can go anywhere without leaving a digital trail, and I'm assuming that's how his assassin tracked him back here. The man who stole the extract is about fifty decks below our feet right now. In the Morgue."

"So his killer has it."

"Who is also in the Morgue. Right beside him."

"So you're not interested in finding the thief…."

"No, I'm looking for the extract. It's gone."

KAT WAS DYING of curiosity by time Jerry returned to their stateroom. From the moment he entered the room she fixed him with a piercing, level stare that seemed to bore into him.

Purely as a matter of perversity, Jerry acted as though he had no clue what was on her mind, and he casually slipped off his shoes and flopped down onto the bed. "Anything to drink in here?" he asked innocently.

Kat hit him with a pillow.

Jerry broke down into giddy laughter as she started pummeling him. "OK, OK, I'll spill the beans! Cease fire!"

He proceeded to repeat to her the whole ugly story, finishing with, "And in retrospect I wish you could have heard it too, because I'm fairly certain that only about half of what he told me is true. There's something else going on here but damned if I can figure it all out yet. I really could have used your Slimlines to stress-check his conversation."

"I think I would have been too disgusted to stay and listen to the whole thing. You men are pathetic – imagine paying a colossal sum and sacrificing lives just to enlarge your –"

"Uh-uh," interrupted Jerry. "No one knows what the guy wants to enlarge. Maybe it's his wife who has body parts she wants to increase in size. Ever think of that?"

"And I'm sure it would be her idea, too."

"Regardless, let's focus on the task at hand. Günter got the gist of the story from the assassin before he died, as well as the personal access code for his data tablet. Apparently the fellow kept meticulous notes; Günter even knows who the buyer is. He can't conduct a search himself because he's under a microscope now, but he can mask our movements and ease our entry into all the places we need to look and when we find it we collect a fat reward.

"Someone will try to kill us, too."

"No, I don't think so. You're looking at this the wrong way. The fellow who stole it while it was in transit to the rich guy – yeah, he was marked for death because he did a bad, bad thing. The superrich don't like to be dicked with. And his murderer got his in a shootout with Günter's pals.

"But us? We're just a third party looking to cash in on a finder's fee. There's no percentage in killing us, there's no revenge or payback motive, we're nothing but yet another helpful resource that is now working in proxy for the rich guy. We can't lose. Either we find it or we don't. No risk."

Kat looked at him with sympathy. She couldn't understand how someone with such a stellar intellect could be so breathtakingly naïve.

*   *   *

"OK, let's recap it one last time."

"Right," replied Jerry, waving his cigar around like a laser pointer ticking off invisible boxes in the air.

"The Prop guy in the theater department, Henryk, was just holding the extract for his brother, the thief who actually stole it from the courier tasked with the delivery. Henryk was going to rendezvous with his sibling at some future port of call and give him back the extract. Then he learned his brother was dead when Stefan, the assassin, tracked him down in the theater and told him."

"Gotcha. And then Stefan tried to bribe Henryk with a pile of cash to tell him where the extract was stashed. But Henryk wouldn't play ball."

"Correctamundo. After pestering Henryk for three days, Stefan lost patience and decided to try a different form of persuasion."

"Which he overdid and ended up accidentally killing Henryk. He panicked when a Security guard coming to lock up the theater for the night saw him with blood all over his shirt and hands, and whom he then shot in the hallway outside the Prop Room before running off."

"Which ultimately resulted in an ill-fated standoff in the passageway."

Jerry leaned back and ran his fingers through his hair. "Which then leads us to that oh-so-lucky bedside conference that Günter shared with Stefan."

"You don't believe it happened the way he said?" asked Kat.

"I don't know *what* to believe in this cockeyed story!

"I don't know where the truth ends and the lies begin – and I know I don't trust Günter. He claims Stefan offered to split the take with him if he could hunt down where Henryk stashed the extract. But then he says Stefan conveniently died just at that moment, after sharing the whole story with him."

"Could Günter kill someone in cold blood?"

"I'm not sure how close Stefan was to death already. He could easily have died all on his own. Or he could have been given a little push – from what I heard, it might not have required much more than pinching his nose shut for 30 seconds. That's not much of a stretch to believe, considering the amount of money we're talking about here."

"Creepy. Gives me the chills. But not enough to make me not want to look for the extract. Where should we begin?"

"Well, Günter's programmed the access keys for Henryk's workshop and living quarters into our ID. He'll cover our tracks in the surveillance system. So I guess we should start in his cabin."

"No time like the present, boss. Let's go."

HENRYK'S QUARTERS were sparse, to say the least. He apparently did little else in his cabin besides watch vids and drink. A lot. There must have been fifty empty liquor bottles in the recycling bin.

"I think Stefan might have done this guy a favour killing him before his liver could explode," said Kat, surveying the jumbled pile of bottles. "How can any one person drink this much?"

"A lot of these itinerant handymen live like this. Unmarried, no real friends, nothing to keep them going but their hose-down in hooch every night. What's impressive is their ability to show up every day and work a full shift. I guess you can do anything with practice."

Kat looked around the room with a discerning eye. Pinching its corner between two fingers, she gingerly lifted a pillow off the end of the couch and peered beneath it. Jerry stepped into the bathroom and inspected the wastebasket and the shower stall.

"This guy doesn't even have a medicine cabinet to look through. The only things in his bathroom are two empty tubes of toothpaste in the wastebasket and a shriveled sliver of soap in the shower. I think we're spinning our wheels here. There's nothing in his quarters. It would be hard to hide even a matchbook in this desert."

"I agree. Let's move this party to the workshop. But I have a question, first."

"Hmm?" responded Jerry, lifting his eyebrows.

"What's 'spinning our wheels' mean?"

Jerry smacked Kat on the butt and strode into the outside corridor. Kat followed, sniggering quietly.

IF HENRYK'S QUARTERS were the desert, they'd landed smack-dab in the middle of the rainforest with his workshop. Every inch of the workspace was cluttered with tools, frames, fabrics, shelves brimming with paraphernalia, and drawers overflowing with nails, screws, hinges and every other building implement known to man.

"Yow, Jerry, we could spend a month searching this place," wailed Kat. "It must have taken years to acquire all this stuff! How are we supposed to sort through it all to find something when we don't even know what it looks like?"

"Look for anything that doesn't belong. It won't be old or dusty. It'll be clean and new and so out of place it will scream out to us."

"Half these drawers don't look like they've even been opened in years. The other half are too full of junk to squeeze in even a paperclip. And there's not even so much as a square inch of free space on the shelves."

"Exactly. Look how many possible hiding spots you've eliminated already."

"What are these?" asked Kat, holding up a stack of flat pans.

Jerry walked over and thought for a moment. "Where did you find them?"

"Over here, on this workbench. It's one of the few spots that looks like it could accommodate some activity."

Jerry pursed his lips and thought for a moment.

"— Oh! I know. These are glass frames. You pour that powder into them." He pointed to a box on the bench, "And you add water, and you get breakaway glass. An actor can crash through it without getting hurt. Like in the vids."

"Oh, I always wondered how they did that," said Kat, putting the trays back.

"Hey! Hold on there!" said Jerry, grabbing the box off the workbench. "Where better to hide something than in a box of powder? Let's pour it out!"

They dumped the entire contents out into a pan, but when they were done there was nothing but a little mountain of grey dust.

"Nothing here," said Jerry. "But look at all the other boxes up there!"

Kat looked up at the top shelf, which was groaning under the weight of at least twenty other boxes of plaster mix, quickcrete, and various other compounds. Kat made a little groan of her own, and then dragged over a chair to start hefting down the boxes while Jerry worked on a similar shelf on the opposite wall.

Forty minutes later, sweating profusely, they stood surrounded by piles of dust and powder of various hues, brushing a fine flour-like coating from their hair and clothes.

Kat grimaced. "*Nothing*. Fuck this guy!"

"Hey hey, let's not speak ill of the dead, Kat."

Kat trained a fish eye on him. "Really?"

Jerry laughed, then said, "Babe, I think we can definitively say there is no extract in here either. Wherever Henryk found to hide his package, he knew better than to choose his workshop or living quarters."

"So where does that leave us?"

"Back at Square One, but listen – if this job were easy, we wouldn't have been hired to do it, now would we?"

"Some consolation. I'm done, old man. Race you to the shower?"

"Shower, yes. Race, no. To tell the truth, I was hoping you'd carry me."

Kat barked out a short hoarse laugh. "Honey, I been carrying you since the day we met," she said with an evil grin.

Before Jerry could respond, she was out the door and cackling her way down the corridor.

CHAPTER XII

JERRY LEANED BACK on the couch and sighed. He chomped down on his cigar and squeezed his eyes shut.

"Günter just sent me a list of Henryk's travels around the ship for the last week. You should check it out. He was a very busy little bee. It could take us a week of our own to follow up on all his activities. I'm starting to regret this assignment."

Kat gave no response, and he looked over to her. She was staring off into space. He watched her eyes darting back and forth behind her Slimlines. "Whatcha doing, hon?" he asked.

"I'm researching this flower, this Goldenroot. There's virtually nothing on the net about it anywhere. I found a single article in a technical medical journal, but most of it is concerned with its molecular properties and such and such. Nothing that could help us."

"Does it say anything at all that a layman might understand?"

"Well, it mentions that the flower smells remarkably similar to Earth's licorice plant. And it says the extract is extremely resistant to temperature changes. It can be frozen, or boiled, or zapped in a microwave, and it stays the same. Pretty weird shit."

"Does that article include a counter to show how many times it's been accessed?" He waited a minute while Kat's eyes flickered around.

"Yeah, there's a counter in the resource stats – it says it's been read twenty-seven times since it was published."

"What about in the last few days, say, since last week?"

Kat paused, then said, "Three times. And I think that includes me."

"Kat baby," said Jerry quietly, rolling his cigar around between his teeth thoughtfully, "I think I might know where the extract could be hidden."

CHAPTER XIII

GÜNTER WATCHED the clock on the wall with a mounting sense of despair. For him, the passage of time was equivalent to the evaporation of his hopes.

He'd been following Jerry's activities around the ship, gradually becoming more and more convinced it was a hopeless task. A ship this size, there were simply an infinite number of places a small package could be hidden away. Especially when it had been held by a person like Henryk, who was technically part of the Maintenance staff and therefore had virtually unrestricted access to almost any area in the ship.

And Henryk had certainly moved around the ship quite a bit in the last week. The man was a frenzy of activity, visiting the storage areas on Decks 6, 7, 9 and 13, the Maintenance Supply Bays at least a dozen times, the Sporting and Shore Excursion depot, Housekeeping, Food Prep, and the Library.

He wasn't sure what he had done in the Library. Surveillance was temporarily down in the Library and there was no rush to get it fixed. It was a low priority among Maintenance tasks. There weren't a lot of crimes committed in the Library.

Besides, the only activities you could engage in there were viewing ancient news vids and using the public terminals to access the net. None of it was important. Günter didn't care what Henryk read or watched. He only wanted to know where he might have stashed the extract.

Günter had an ace up his sleeve, though, that he didn't share with Jerry.

He'd discovered an obscure scientific journal on the net and had downloaded a spec sheet of the basic chemical composition of the extract.

While there were several unknown and indecipherable compounds in the extract, some of them were universally recognized.

Günter had programmed the ship's environmental sensors to sniff out that specific combination of known compounds. As long as the package wasn't hermetically sealed, as soon as it was exposed to the air anywhere on the ship Günter would get an emergency alert delivered to him alone.

He was mulling over what his next step should be when his commlink chimed. He tapped his ear and said, "Klum."

"Günter, it's Jerome. I need an access code."

"To what?"

"To an airlock. So I can go outside."

"Why in the world would you want to do that?"

"It's just a hunch. If it pays off, you'll be the first to know."

"Uh-huh. I dunno, Jerome. That's a real touchy one. If I give you a code and it goes south for you out there, they won't stop at just firing me. They'll tear my head right off and shit directly down my throat."

"Nice image, Gun. Look, you want to find this thing or not? I need to go outside."

Long sigh.

"Fine. I'll send you the code. But airlock codes are one-time-use only."

"In that case, send me two. I might need a backup."

"Alright, but watch your ass out there, Jerome. Losing a passenger to vacuum would be the icing on the cake for me."

"I'm touched by your concern. I'll wait for those codes."

ERRY, ARE YOU going to tell me why we need to go outside the ship, or are you going to keep it to yourself?”

“Calm down, Kat. I’m still working this out myself – look, it’s that technical sheet you found. Did anything jump out at you?”

“Honestly, most of it was over my head. All I remember was that it smells like licorice.”

“Aaaaand… it’s impervious to temperature. It can be frozen or boiled or zapped, and nothing hurts or changes it.”

“Sooooo…?”

“So what environment offers extreme temperatures?”

“Outer space!”

“Precisely! And I’ll bet Henryk was one of the two other people who read that technical article on Goldenroot this week.”

“I’m starting to think he was more than just a washed-out drunk. And he worked in Maintenance so he had access to the airlocks and the access codes. What better place to hide something from prying eyes than somewhere that no one ever goes?”

“So it must be in a magnetic box attached to the hull somewhere? Awesome! We can go outside and scan for magnetic objects and find it in seconds!” Kat was excited now, and her eyes sparkled as she sensed the end of their hunt.

“Well, that’s not precisely true. It might just be sitting out there somewhere. In fact, it probably isn’t in a magnetic case for exactly the reason you just mentioned – it would be too easy to scan for.”

"But then how would you secure it in place? It could just float away!"

"No, Kat. Gravity doesn't just *end* when you step outside the ship. The outer hull of most starships is covered with space junk, tiny micrometeors, and various discarded detritus from the humans who've passed across their surface.

"Tools don't need to be magnetic to stay put any more than tools on Earth or on any other planet. This ship has its own gravity well, tiny though it may be. While the hull does block a good deal of the ship's gravity, enough leaks through that there's still a pretty significant pull out there."

"So what you're saying is, if I want to hide something from the onboard sensors and security staff, I can just dump it wherever I want on the hull and it'll stay there?"

"Well, yes, but within reason.

"Again, pretend you're on a planet. There's an orientation to gravity's pull – you can't set something on a wall or ceiling. Or even on a tilted surface.

"The same rules apply here. Even outside the ship, there's an 'up' and a 'down'. And whatever you leave behind better be securely snug in place, or it'll get jostled loose during sub-lightspeed maneuvering."

"What about during lightspeed?"

"There's no inertia during lightspeed – we're not moving, only the graviton bubble we're enclosed in is moving. Hence, no feeling of movement, no inertia, no crushing g-force, etc."

"Then that narrows down our search by a lot. The package has to be somewhere on the "top" of the ship."

"And not where anyone would see it from a viewport, or where anyone might stumble across it during routine maintenance."

"So what does that leave us?"

Jerry leaned over a tabletop hologram of the ship that Günter had sent him and started circling wide swaths of area.

"Not here…" he said, drawing a raggedy circle around an area forward of the Bridge then blacking it out, "Not here, where the electrical conduit access ports are located, not around the observation domes or shuttle bays…."

He continued circling areas until he straightened back up and said, "There. Somewhere in this central zone."

Kat looked dubiously at what remained.

"That's quite a lot of area to search when we don't even know what we're looking for among all the other random crap that's collected on the hull," she said.

Jerry shook his head.

"Our package will be clean, and snugly stowed. It will be obvious exactly *because* of its non-random appearance.

"That's what will give it away."

KAT FINISHED SLITHERING into her snugsuit and glanced up at Jerry's face. He was watching her closely with obvious pleasure.

"Good God, Jerry, wipe that grin off your face. Do you ever stop thinking about sex?"

Jerry chuckled and leaned over to plant a kiss on her cheek. "Baby, you can hardly blame me for appreciating what you look like while you wrap yourself up in that second skin. It's one of my favourite shows."

She sighed, then grinned back at him. "I guess I can't say I'm not appreciated. I just wish it weren't always for my body, though."

"Hey, I love your mind, too! I just can't see your mind. This I can see." And he reached out and squeezed one of her breasts.

Laughing, Kat smacked his hand away and barked, "Hands off, mister! Focus on the job!"

Sighing dramatically, Jerry turned away and plucked her helmet from the top shelf of the closet.

"These three mini canisters on the back are good for ten minutes each. That's thirty minutes max, got it?"

"We've been over this, Jerry."

"I just don't want you losing track of time, OK?"

"Slimlines, Jerry! Remember?" said Kat, tapping her finger against her glasses. "I'm not wearing these for the fashion statement you know."

"Yeah yeah, I get it. But I don't believe in relying so much on technology. Shit happens. Machines fail. You need to pay attention out there. You count on those things too much."

"These '*things*' have saved my ass more times than I can remember. Damn right I count on them."

"That's fine. Just don't lose track of time and space. Your glasses can't die. You can."

Immediately, they both fell silent. The seriousness of what Kat was attempting suddenly weighed down on them. Jerry was upset she was going out instead of him but they'd decided only one of them should be outdoors at a time, and Kat had won the coin toss.

Jerry had protested, but Kat was hearing none of it. She had no patience with this "weaker sex bullshit", as she put it.

They'd carefully examined the holo display of the ship's schematics. There were eleven possible airlocks on the upper decks, and they'd whittled down their choices by cross-referencing Henryk's movements through the ship in his final week.

He'd stopped in at the Sporting and Shore Excursions depot and there was an airlock in their storage bay, probably to facilitate the frequent return of various dirty or contaminated equipment that passengers had taken off-ship. They had no idea whether Henryk had been there to access the airlock or for another reason entirely, but he had come by late at night so they figured it was a likely choice.

Additionally, the section was closed after hours, so there were no prying eyes for Jerry and Kat to avoid. Günter had added a carte-blanche access code to their ID and the doors swept open for them at their approach.

Kat took her helmet from Jerry, quickly checked to make sure the oxygen canisters were secure, then slipped it over her head. A soft click indicated the seal had been made. She was ready to go.

Kat saw Jerry's lips moving and she tapped the side of her helmet. Jerry stopped talking, then pressed a button on his lapel.

"Sorry. Am I coming in loud and clear now?"

"Yep, and I better get moving. No point in wasting air."

And Kat turned and stepped into the airlock, closed it behind her, and stood facing the outer door while the airlock cycled down.

THE AIRLOCK OPENED onto a wide docking platform, and off to one side a small gate gave access to a long narrow metal gangway on the side of the ship. At various intervals along the gangway's length were ladders stretching up the hull. Kat looked down, and below her she could see the bulge of the viewing dome protruding from the side of the ship.

The entire ship was bathed in light pouring out from the thousands of viewports along its sides. Evidently, almost every cabin was currently occupied as the passengers were all busy changing into evening wear and getting ready to go to dinner.

And here I am, skulking along outside like some shady burglar, thought Kat. *Some lousy vacation I get. Typical!*

Quickly, she scurried over to the nearest ladder and began the climb up to the top deck. It was easier than she'd thought it would be. *There may be gravity out here, but it's pretty weak. I'll have to be careful.* She glanced to her side at the endless inky darkness around her. *That's a pretty long fall....*

When she reached the top of the ladder Kat could see wide strips of metal stretching away out of sight, like long sidewalks pasted across the ship's ceramic hull. Her Slimlines automatically switched on her magnetic boots and Kat ran effortlessly along the path. Coupled with the weak gravity, it made for a smooth, effortless running experience and Kat was soon smack dab in the middle of the upper hull. Now she was in almost complete darkness, surrounded on all sides by silent shadowy shapes.

Kat told her Slimlines to present the view to her as a daylight scene. The image snapped to life immediately in full-spectrum colour as the Slimlines translated their IR-LIDAR imaging into normal human sight perception.

All around her were hundreds of protrusions, antennae, heat sinks, access ports, sensors and various mechanical contrivances scattered in seeming disarray, as though the builders had let machines and equipment drop completely randomly.

She looked over sharply to her right, where a small pile of trash sat glittering under a cooling port. Stepping off the metal walkway, she unconsciously held her breath in anticipation of floating away into the void, but exhaled in relief when she felt the ship's gravity holding her down.

"This is creepy, Jerry. I feel like at any moment I could drift off this thing."

Normally, her suit would have reproduced his voice in perfectly modulated tones. It should have sounded as though he were standing at her side, but instead the sound crackled and popped faintly when he replied back. A few syllables dropped out.

"Keep it together, baby," came his fuzzy response.

Jerry was trying to sound soothing and confident, even though he was probably more on edge than she was.

"Play it safe and you'll be back in no time. You see anything yet?"

"There's some trash here off to the side, but I think it's just leftover garbage from some work crew."

"Look for something out of place, something that doesn't belong. It's probably in a place easy to get to – you'd want to be able to retrieve it without too much trouble or traveling."

Kat looked across the expanse of ship before her. Notwithstanding the zones they had eliminated from the search, what remained looked like it would take days to properly survey.

Unless….

Kat clicked her front teeth together and said to her Slimlines, "Scan. Identify every item in the display. Remove all objects associated with the ship's operation. Highlight all others."

Immediately the entire surface of the ship appeared to Kat as a black, featureless vista with faint grey translucent shapes replacing each of the multitude of objects. Here and there a small green dot was highlighted.

She studied the view for a minute, then ran over to a central metal "sidewalk" traversing the length of the ship and began to jog rapidly along the path, darting her glance from left to right as she went.

When she came level with a green dot she'd quickly foray over to it, only to discover bits and pieces of old satellites, chunks of asteroids, and random pieces of equipment discarded by old work crews.

She kept returning to the main central walkway and admonished her Slimlines to be more discriminating in their selection. She wanted only manmade objects that didn't belong out in space.

She hadn't gone more than fifty meters when a bright green dot off to her right made her stop in her tracks.

"I think we've got something, Jerry. I'm going into – " she checked the readout in a corner of her vision – "Into grid four-nine-Alpha."

She paused, waiting for his acknowledgement.

"Jerry?"

Nothing.

A faint hiss of static bled through her helmet commlink, and Kat glanced around at all the unshielded equipment on the hull.

The electrical interference and transmission signals must be intense up here. I hope I'm not sterilizing myself.

She stepped off the metal pathway and the static crackled painfully in her ear.

Well, guess I'm really on my own now, and with a tap of her teeth she switched off the commlink.

Kat reset the view to show all objects clearly so she didn't accidentally walk into a power bank or trip over a conduit. But the green glowing dot turned out to be nothing more than a small sack containing some mountain-climbing gear.

Climbing the thousands of asteroids, moons and planets scattered throughout the galaxy was a favourite sport for those who wanted a challenge that Earth couldn't offer. The sack had probably tumbled free from a shore excursion shuttle with a loose cargo bay door.

Kat glanced at the readout in the corner of her display. She'd used up eleven minutes of air. Still plenty of time left.

She turned and started heading back to the walkway but got only about five paces when something in the back of her brain made her stop and look back at the sack.

It was laying snugly tucked away on a natural shelf formed where a meter-square sensor box pushed up against a larger generator unit. It looked too perfect to have fallen there by accident. And after all, Henryk did visit the Sporting and Shore Excursion depot last week. He might have left this sack here to use on a return visit.

Kat slowly looked around her and focused on each of the shapes in the area.

Not very far away a group of tall spires were clumped together, rising about five meters above the hull. Probably an antenna array or transmitting unit of some kind.

"Zoom. Scan each of those pillars. What do you see that's not right?"

Immediately her glasses zeroed in on a closed panel near the top of one spire; one edge of the access cover looked slightly ajar, as though something inside were pushing it out of alignment.

Kat ran over to the sack and upended it on the sensor box unit. She ignored the coil of climbing rope and the crampons and carabiners, and selected a short positioning lanyard with handles at either end.

Running over to the spire, she reached around the base and grabbed an end of the lanyard in one hand and drew it around the backside. By pulling it tight around the spire she was able shinny up bit by bit, holding her position by clamping her knees tight against either side of the pillar while she moved the lanyard up higher and higher.

Thank God for low gravity, she thought.

And Thank God Jerry's not here to see this – she could only imagine the comments he would be making.

Grunting with the effort and feeling her suit wick the perspiration off her body, she was only slightly annoyed when her Slimlines gently reminded her "50% of air remaining, Kat."

Well, she thought, if this hunch was correct she'd be back inside even before the third canister was needed.

As she reached the top, the panel drew even with her face.

Kat leaned back to get a clear look, and sure enough, there was definitely something wrong with it – she pressed the cover into place and it bulged outward again. She looked at the closure and grimaced to see that it had a funky release slot, probably intended for some special tool.

But Kat had her own 'special' tools. She was wearing a tool belt that she had liberated from Henryk's workshop. She drew out a short pry bar with a nasty sharp flat hook at one end.

She stuck the hook into the gap in the panel closure, and yanked.

The door popped open so readily it almost sent Kat tumbling from her perch, but she clamped her knees together even tighter around the spire and she quickly regained her balance.

Unfortunately, whatever it was that had been stuffed inside the panel must have accidentally hooked onto the door because when the hatch's cover burst open the package flung itself off into space past her shoulder in a long gentle arc, spinning end over end toward the side of the ship.

"Damn!" howled Kat, watching helplessly as the little package tumbled silently through the vacuum.

What with the lack of atmosphere to slow its path, and the weak gravity that barely affected it at its current height of about ten meters above the ship, the package looked like it would miss the outer edge of the hull by several meters before sailing off into space.

No no no no no, thought Kat frantically.

She dropped the pry bar and threw herself off the spire, gracefully flipping backwards to land on her feet and breaking into a run as soon as her boots gained traction.

Leaping over some obstacles and pushing off against others, she flung herself across the hull, one eye on her path and the other on the package spinning away above her.

When it was still about three meters away from her she carefully judged her distance and its trajectory, and she leapt.

It was a perfect leap.

She sailed up in silent flight and grasped the package firmly in her outstretched right hand, crying "Gotcha!" as she nabbed it, and only then did she notice the edge of the ship disappearing behind her as her leap continued to carry her up and over the side.

Into space.

JERRY HAD WASTED no time slipping into his own snugsuit immediately after Kat had exited the airlock door.

He was glad she'd insisted that he buy himself a new suit, and despite his embarrassment at the skintight fabric outlining every bulge and protrusion on his body, he enjoyed the sleek experience of moving in it.

Kat would have been livid if she'd known he was suiting up, and would have wasted precious time and energy carping about his lack of confidence in her. But if all went well, he could be out of his suit and into his clothes again before she made it back through the airlock. No harm being prepared, though.

The audio had failed on their commlink, but Kat's Slimlines were still transmitting a fuzzy video image.

He nervously followed her progress across the hull and up the spire in his helmet's display. As she jumped down from the spire and chased the package across the ship, he held his breath. And when she leapt up and over the side of the ship, he gasped in horror.

KAT WATCHED THE ship disappear past her feet. But she was moving slowly enough that she wasn't too panicked. First, she quickly tucked away her precious package in a chest pouch. Then she reached down to her tool belt and drew out a hammer. It had a satisfying heft in her hand.

Considering her trajectory carefully, Kat gritted her teeth and threw the hammer as hard as she could into deep space. It worked.

Her momentum immediately slowed to almost nothing, and she began a slow graceful spin in place, about fifteen meters past the edge of the hull.

She drew a pair of pliers from her belt. Lighter than the hammer, but significant nonetheless. She paused, then flung them after the hammer.

The pliers must have weighed more than Kat had thought because they really gave her a boost. Unfortunately, it was in the wrong direction.

Her slow spin had thrown off her aim, and now she was in a gentle tumble and heading up, not down. Still fifteen meters from the ship.

This was not good. She was running out of things to throw.

She pulled out a couple of screwdrivers and tossed them opposite where she hoped to end up, but this was getting more complicated by the minute. Her tumbling was getting worse and the screwdrivers had barely enough mass to move her anywhere at all.

She took off the tool belt and thought carefully.

She waited until her orientation was precisely where she wanted it, and flung the belt. Unfortunately, being flexible, it didn't leave her hand cleanly, but curled around itself and her hand before spinning away.

And sent her back out into space away from the ship.

This was really bad now.

Kat had nothing left to throw but her boots or gloves. While her wrist and ankle cuffs would maintain the suit's integrity, losing the boots or gloves would mean freezing her feet or hands solid. Not a good option.

There was one last thing to try. Her last chance.

She blew out a long strong stream of air from her lungs, then inhaled deeply. Then she did it again. When her lungs were full to bursting, she twisted the third air canister off the back of her helmet and held it out in front of her.

Locating the manual release, she waited until her orientation was just right, then briefly pressed down on the valve. A burst of snowy white air shot out into space.

It was stronger than she'd dared hope. It had the dual effect of slowing her tumbling action and pushing her back towards the ship.

She aimed again, and shot again. Now she definitely had momentum. She started coasting back and down towards the ship.

Excited, she pressed the valve again.

Oops. Too much downward momentum. The ship's gravity must be tugging her back down now that she was closer to the superstructure. She was going to hit the hull too hard.

She didn't want to break an ankle landing; she needed to get inside quickly before she suffocated.

She risked a glance at her heads-up display. Good. She had just over a minute of air in the internal emergency reserve.

She aimed the canister again, but slightly downwards this time, and fired a short burst.

It seemed like the kick from the valve was a little weaker. It was probably getting near empty. And while the puff of air slowed her descent, she had also inadvertently angled her approach and increased her lateral momentum. Now she was floating almost parallel to the ship, still on a collision course, but moving high and hard alongside it toward the stern.

She looked over her shoulder at the hull. She was three-quarters of the way down the length of the ship. Last hurrah here.

She pressed down on the valve and watched the last of the air stream out in what she hoped was the best direction to drive her far away from the edge. She craned her neck around and was gratified to see the hull beneath her and coming up fast.

She was going to impact the ship about ten meters in from the top edge.

Perfect.

She readied herself for landing, prepared to jam her boots down onto the hull at maximum strength. Her suit would release before she could injure herself, but the initial contact would most surely kill all her forward momentum.

When she hit, it was like falling out of a moving car.

The impact knocked the wind out of her and she began rolling and bouncing uncontrollably. There were no walkways down at this end of the hull. There was nothing for the magnets in her boots to grip onto.

She tumbled across the smooth ceramic surface which suddenly became startlingly transparent as she passed over the clear ceiling of one of the aft restaurants. *Eat under the stars!* she remembered the promotional vid boasting. Quick staccato images of diners seated below her flashed across her vision as she bounced end over end across the restaurant's roof. She wondered peripherally if any of the diners were shocked to see her flailing form tumble across the vista above their heads.

And then she was back bouncing and rolling on the smooth ceramic surface of the hull. There was still nothing to slow her down as she drew closer and closer to the stern of the huge starship.

And then, even worse, she noticed that the surface was gradually curving "downward", as the gentle arcing lines that had so pleased the esthetics of the ship's designers compounded her trajectory.

The combination of the ship's gravity and the declining angle of the hull continued to accelerate her passage. Kat found, though, that by splaying her arms and legs out spread-eagle she could slow her tumbling, and finally she found herself face down against the hull, sliding at breakneck speed at a greater and greater downward angle as she coursed along the slick ceramic surface.

She craned her neck to peer ahead, hoping to spot a projection or lip or anything she could grab hold of. But all she saw was a fast-approaching unending vista of pitch-black darkness spread out in front of her.

I hope I die, she thought grimly. *Because if I don't Jerry will never let me forget this.*

CHAPTER XIX

IF HE HADN'T had to wait for the airlock to cycle down, Jerry could have made it up onto the hull while Kat was still within reach, but he was only just emerging from the access port when he saw her form whiz past toward the ship's stern.

He threw himself up the ladder, careful not to jostle loose the equipment slung on his back, and winced as he saw her helpless form smash down on the hull and start to tumble away down its length.

He began running after her at what he considered a pretty good clip, but she was moving so much faster than him the gap between them grew at exponential amounts every few seconds.

He cleared the restaurant roof in one tremendous leap, and then he noticed his own speed was increasing as well. The declination in the hull coupled with the ship's gravity began to assist his momentum until he was more bounding than running. He could still see Kat ahead of him, sliding on her face now, but she was about to disappear over the lip of the ship.

Jerry reached down within himself and dredged up every bit of energy he possessed, throwing himself with as much strength as he could muster down and along the hull, until he too lost all control and slid over the edge.

He floated ever so gently away from the ship's superstructure in a smooth free fall through the vacuum. He could see Kat's form far below him, gently turning end over end against the indigo of space.

He reached over his shoulder and pulled free the speargun he'd strapped to his back. Holding his breath, he let the tiny laser dot settle on Kat, waited until her retreating form had rotated into position, and he pulled the trigger.

The recoil from the bolt pushed him violently backwards, but he wasn't worried about the arrow missing Kat; the harpoon was laser guided once it left the gun. It would self-correct its trajectory to pierce its victim exactly where the dot had been placed. Behind it, a thin stream of nanofiber cable snaked out all the way back to the tether attached to his waist.

Without looking to see the result of his shot, Jerry reached up and pulled out another spear from his backpack.

Twisting his torso and pausing to accommodate the slight rotation his first shot had given him, he sighted the nest of conduits and hosing surrounding the docking stations on the underside of the ship.

Carefully fixing his targeting laser on the thickest bundle of cables, he shot the bolt and grunted in satisfaction as it buried itself into the nest of cables.

The tethers attaching the harpoons to his suit were made with special elastic properties. Their original intention had been to cushion spearfishermen from the jolt of their prey's thrashing, but they served equally well to absorb most of the snap as they arrested his momentum and held him in place.

Satisfied they weren't going to drift away, Jerry turned his attention back to Kat. Better reel her in.

And boy, is she going to be *pissed.*

WHEN HER SUIT'S air had run out, and then the power shut down, Kat had momentarily panicked. Then, she relaxed. *It is what it is*, she thought placidly. *Not how I wanted to go out, but no sense raging against the dying of the light. Embrace it, Kat.*

Then she felt the most God-awful crescendo of pain cascade through her left calf. It was as though she'd stepped on an unshielded electrical cable and seared off her whole leg.

"FUUUUUUUUUUUUUUCK!" she screamed.

What the shit just happened? Am I dead already and in Hell?!

Then another jolt, and the pain grew worse.

And then, blessedly, she passed out from lack of air.

CHAPTER XXI

JERRY REELED IN Kat at top speed. He pulled so fast her body crashed into him at over twenty miles an hour. But he held on tight then looked inside her helmet. She didn't look dead, but she didn't look alive either. He spun her around to check the back of her helmet and saw that the third oxygen canister was missing.

Without pausing, he reached down and yanked a hose cable out from his hip and jammed it into a socket on Kat's suit. Her helmet filled with air and the suit's internal lights illuminated as it rebooted.

The comm light started blinking as it connected with Jerry's suit.

But she still wasn't breathing.

"Come on, Kat! I can't give you mouth to mouth while floating in space!"

Jerry spun her so her back was to him and stretched his arms around her, then clasped his hands together just beneath her sternum. Pumping and squeezing her stomach and chest, he tried to simulate the movements of her breathing.

After a dozen compressions, he felt a soft cough. He spun her around and was thrilled to see her eyes flutter open.

Her suit transmitted a raspy breath and then she said, "God, Jerry, what the hell happened? I feel like I stepped in a bear trap!"

He looked down at the spear buried in her leg.

"Long story, babe. I'll have to tell you when we're inside."

And he started reeling them back up toward the ship.

THE WOUND WAS less serious than Jerry had even dared hope. Turns out, the ship's medical crew saw spearfishing accidents more frequently than anyone wanted to admit, and they'd grown quite good at extracting the thin harpoons and sealing the puncture points.

Kat was lucky that the bolt had miraculously passed through her calf between her tibia and fibula, sparing her broken bones and serious damage. Also fortunately, the ice-cold bolt had virtually cauterized the wound and prevented almost all blood loss. And her snugsuit's automatic compression around the entry point had prevented any oxygen necrosis. There was a slight tear in the muscle, and she'd have a little dimple scar at the entry and exit points, but other than that, almost no damage.

"And the best idea you could think of was to *shoot* me," muttered Kat, sitting in her underwear on the bed in their stateroom, eyeing Jerry evilly as she gingerly applied a healing salve to her wound.

"Hey," replied Jerry. "You use the tools you're given. I was standing in the Sporting Depot. Tennis rackets and volleyballs weren't looking like a very good option. Just be happy you'd allowed me to drag my suit along with me."

"Yeah yeah, I suppose I should be *thanking* you," she grumbled, but Jerry could see her eyes tearing up. He leaned close and hugged her and she melted into his arms.

"Thank you for saving me yet again, Jerry," she whispered into his neck, teardrops dripping down her cheek and onto his shoulder.

"Let's not make it a habit, though, babe," whispered Jerry, trying to hold it together himself.

"Hey!" barked Kat suddenly, pushing Jerry back, wiping her eyes and straightening out her hair. "To the task at hand! Have you opened up that damned package yet?"

"To tell the truth, I've had other things on my mind recently, but now that you mention it let's take a look."

Jerry snatched Kat's snugsuit up from the floor and pulled open the storage pouch on the front. Inside was a small fabric sack with a zipper closure. Jerry unzipped it and drew out a flat plastic box sealed at one end with heavy tape.

"Hold your breath, baby, this looks like paydirt," he said, setting the box down on a writing desk. He leaned down to his duffel bag on the floor and rooted around in it for a few seconds, then pulled out a pair of work gloves. "Don't want to end up with sausage fingers," he chuckled, and then slit the tape with a letter opener from the desk drawer.

He gently tapped the open end of the box against his palm and out slid two white glass vials capped with rubbery black stoppers. The smell of licorice immediately filled the room. He popped the tops off the vials and out from each slid a little cylindrical clear plastic tube of white ointment. Jerry pushed the empty vials aside and said, "Bingo."

Kat sucked in her breath. She'd hobbled over to the desk to watch. The plastic tubes of creamy extract sat dully on the desk, and for a moment it was almost an underwhelming sight, after all they'd been through to get them. But then she realized what they represented, and her pulse quickened again.

JERRY CHEWED THOUGHTFULLY on the end of his cigar and idly pushed the little tubes around on the desk with a pencil. He had an envelope prepared with Günter's name on it and he was getting ready to seal one of the tubes of extract in it and send it up to him, but he was puzzling over what to do with his own.

He put down his cigar and picked up one of the tiny cylinders, letting it rest in the palm of his gloved hand. Then he shook his head again and put it back down.

"What's troubling you, Jer?" asked Kat, watching his face.

"Well baby, the problem as I see it, now that we've found these little bastards, is how to get one off the ship safely. No way will I pack it up in my luggage for Security to scan. God only knows how many people know about this cluster-fuck by now. I wouldn't be surprised if half the Ship's Staff were waiting to strip-search us as we debark.

"And I can't carry it off on my person – even the most cursory body scan will tip them to any package I carry.

"So what to do…." Jerry reached down and picked up his cigar to chew on meditatively, but no sooner had he put it in his mouth than he jerked it out and spluttered. "Ack! What the –" And he saw that in his inattention he'd accidentally picked up one of the empty glass vials instead and put it in his mouth.

"Whoa. That surprised me. Through the gloves that vial felt just like my ciga –

"KAT! That's it! My cigar!"

Kat looked at him patiently. She'd been through this kind of thought process before with Jerry. In a minute he would begin to make sense. She just had to give him time to order his thoughts coherently enough to express them.

"Don't you see? My cigar is the answer!

"The tube of extract will fit perfectly inside my cigar, if I just slit a tiny hole in the side and hollow out a small cavity. And the compound is heat-resistant, so I can even have the cigar lit while the tube's in there! It's perfect! The bioscans won't see the compound inside the cigar because it's all organic, and the superheated air will mess with any IR scan. I can walk right off the ship waving the extract under their noses!"

It was precisely at that moment that their stateroom door swung open and Günter strolled in, closing the door behind him.

"Congratulations, Jerome," he said cheerily. "That sounds like an excellent idea. But I'm curious – do you think you could fit *both* of those little packets into one cigar? I'm only asking because…."

And his voice trailed off as he lifted a hand from his jacket pocket and pointed a small weapon at the couple standing at the desk.

CHAPTER XXIV

BARELY AN HOUR ago, Günter had been sitting at his workstation staring at a blank screen. His monitor was off, but his mind was working at a million miles an hour.

He could tell that Jerome had an inkling where the package was hidden. The request for airlock codes might have been just a red herring, so Jerome could come back to Günter and say 'Sorry old boy, I came up empty', and then stroll off the ship with the package. OR… maybe the package *was* outside, and Jerome had tracked it down.

But if that were true, could Günter trust Jerome to admit he'd found it?

What was there to keep Jerome from vamoosing with the goods and leaving Günter hanging out in the breeze?

His head hurt.

Just then an alert chimed in his ear and he tapped his desk display for the report. Ah. Jerome's woman had needed to visit the med bay after suffering a spearfishing accident.

Spearfishing? But he'd just seen barely one hour ago that both airlock codes he'd given them had been used. What in the world were these two up to?

Günter was just about to call Jerome and demand some answers when an entirely different and much more urgent alert illuminated his whole display.

The compound had just been detected in the ship!

In Jerome's stateroom, in fact!

Günter rubbed his hands together in glee. This had just gone from a very bad day to a most excellent one, indeed.

He cleared his display, wiped the alerts from the system, and wiped all of Jerry's enhanced ID permissions.

He deleted all the surveillance records of Henryk and then everything the system had on the Weasel.

Especially the Weasel, he thought.

Killing him had been oh so easy, but he still didn't want any records left in the system that would link the two of them together. The ship's Management would be happy to see he'd wiped all the records – it would help them blunt any investigations and make it that much harder for any relatives to sue.

Once he was off the ship – *which should be about thirty minutes from now,* he thought, checking his watch – this whole mess would be nothing but a bad memory for him. But one with a glorious payday at the end.

Günter stood up and leisurely stretched while he looked around the room. He couldn't pretend he would miss this sorry sight.

He glanced at the woman sitting opposite.

Yep, her left eye had definitely developed a twitch.

He turned and strode out of the room for the last time and headed down the corridor towards the armory. After all, he couldn't very well show up at Jerome's stateroom empty-handed.

JERRY AND KAT stared silently at Günter and the little weapon in his right hand. The implication was fairly obvious.

"You don't need to do this, Günter," said Jerry. "Look, I've already got your envelope ready for your share. We can both come out of this deal much richer."

"You're already rich, Jerome," replied Günter sourly. "But now I have no job and no prospects – no one in the known galaxies will ever hire me after this affair. I'd be lucky to find a job digging ditches.

"It really ticks me off," he continued, growing more animated, "To always be treated like I'm an idiot.

"*'Not suited for piloting work; recommend maintenance dept.'* – that's what Deep Space Transports wrote in my file. *'Not suited for field work; recommend desk position'* – that one was from Kobar Private Investigations. *'Not suited for tractor work; recommend harvesting and baling'* – that was in my FarmCorps file.

"*NOT SUITED FOR TRACTOR WORK*, Jerome!" Günter screamed, bringing his face close to Jerry's. "They don't even think I'm smart enough to drive a fucking *TRACTOR!*"

"Okaaaay," offered Jerry quietly, "So maybe heavy equipment isn't your thi—"

Günter backhanded Jerry in the mouth with his gun and Jerry spun around and fell off the chair.

"Save your condescension. I'm done with all of you. This is *my* time, now."

He dragged Jerry over to the middle of the room and sat him on the floor, then tied him back-to-back with Kat.

Jerry was bleeding from his mouth where Günter had hit him and his lip was swelling up and turning scarlet red.

Günter picked up from the desk the envelope that Jerry had prepared for him and carefully swept in the two pouches of extract, and then slipped it into his jacket's inside breast pocket.

"I am walking right off this ship with this envelope in my pocket," he said with smug satisfaction. "I don't get scanned, so don't worry about me.

"You two should have no trouble untying yourselves in the next twenty minutes or so, and I'd recommend you vamoose from this ship as soon as you can. I have a feeling things are going to start unraveling pretty damn quick. But by then, I should be looooong gone. The spaceport where we're currently docked has flights leaving every thirty seconds for every corner of the galaxy. I'm sure I can find a seat on one of them.

"Thanks for your help, and *arrivederci*, my friend. I hope you enjoyed your stay on the *Buona Fortuna* – I'll tell you, it sure turned out pretty *buona* for me."

"Günter," croaked Jerry, still bleeding and lisping slightly through his bruised and swollen lip, "Günter, don't try to thell that thtuff – they'll kill you."

"Yeah, thanks for the advice, '*partner*', I think I can take care of myself. But it's nice to know you still care."

And so saying, he walked out of the stateroom and straight toward Gangway Number Seven, currently discharging guests into the spaceport.

"**G**OTTA SAY, Jerry, your choice of friends leaves a little something to be desired," muttered Kat as they worked the knots on each other's wrists.

"I never thedd I truthted the guy," lisped Jerry.

As soon as they'd untied themselves both Jerry and Kat bustled through the stateroom, stuffing their belongings into their bags.

Jerry swept his cigar and gloves and the empty glass vials and everything else off the desk and into his duffel bag and Kat ran a final check, looking under the bed and in the closets.

"OK, that's everything," she said. "Let's hit the road. Fast."

"Sure," replied Jerry, "But I want to stop in at that little candy store on the Promenade and pick up some of their Italian licorice – after smelling it for the last hour I've got a bit of a craving. It won't take a sec."

THEY MADE IT through Debarkation Screening without a hitch and soon found themselves safely back on their ship, speeding away from the huge starship.

The swelling in Jerry's wounded lip had mostly subsided but it was still just a bit puffy, and gave him some trouble pronouncing "s". Other than that and the stiffness in Kat's calf from her puncture wound, they were none the worse for wear. They put the ship on autopilot and settled down onto the couch in the lounge with two exhausted sighs of relief.

Jerry dumped out the contents of his duffel onto the coffee table in their lounge area and immediately the whole chamber was filled with the pungent smell of licorice. Jerry's recent purchases were scattered across the table: licorice drops, licorice extract, licorice twists – there was an extensive collection.

"That Security guy thought your candy collection was pretty funny, Jer," said Kat, wrinkling her nose at the strong aroma as it filled the air.

"That's what I was hoping, Kat," replied Jerry thoughtfully.

She looked at him with raised eyebrows and then said slowly, "OK, buster. Spill it. Let me in on what evil thoughts are coursing through that grey matter of yours."

Jerry turned to her and said carefully, "Kat, did anything about Henryk's cabin bother you? Anything seem not right?"

"You mean, besides the year's collection of empty liquor bottles in the recycler?"

"No, not that. Kat – do you remember I saw two empty toothpaste tubes in the bathroom wastebasket?"

"Um, yeah…. Is that strange to you?"

"Only when there's no toothbrush present."

Slowly, a dawning recognition crept across Kat's face.

"Jerry!" she whispered, "The tubes of white paste that Günter grabbed! You're not saying –"

"Uh-huh. I think those tubes were decoys. To mess with anyone who thought they'd found the compound. That's why I tried to warn Günter not to sell them. Someone's going to get real pissed off when they rub toothpaste all over their –"

"But then where's the real deal?" interrupted Kat.

Jerry leaned over to the table, and picking up a licorice twist, he carefully slid it into one of the empty glass vials and lifted it up to Kat's face.

"Remember Henryk had that powder for making fake glass?" he asked softly. Kat's eyes grew to the size of saucers.

"It came to me while Günter was tying us up.

"When I accidentally stuck one of these vials in my mouth instead of my cigar I tasted licorice. I didn't peg to it right away, but I noticed a few minutes later that my tongue felt funny, like it was just a bit swollen. Or slightly larger."

"I thought you were lisping because Günter smacked you in the kisser!"

"Mostly, I was. But not only because of that."

"So how do we get the extract back?"

"Easy-peasy. We heat up the vials in the microwave and melt them back to liquid form. What's left is our retirement fund."

"Ooooh, Jerry! I *knew* I loved you for more than just your good looks!"

"Har-de-har. Wanna go warm these babies up?"

"Not just yet, honey," said Kat with a wicked grin, standing up and taking Jerry by the hand. "I think we need to visit the bedroom first. Didn't you say something about a slightly larger tongue…?"

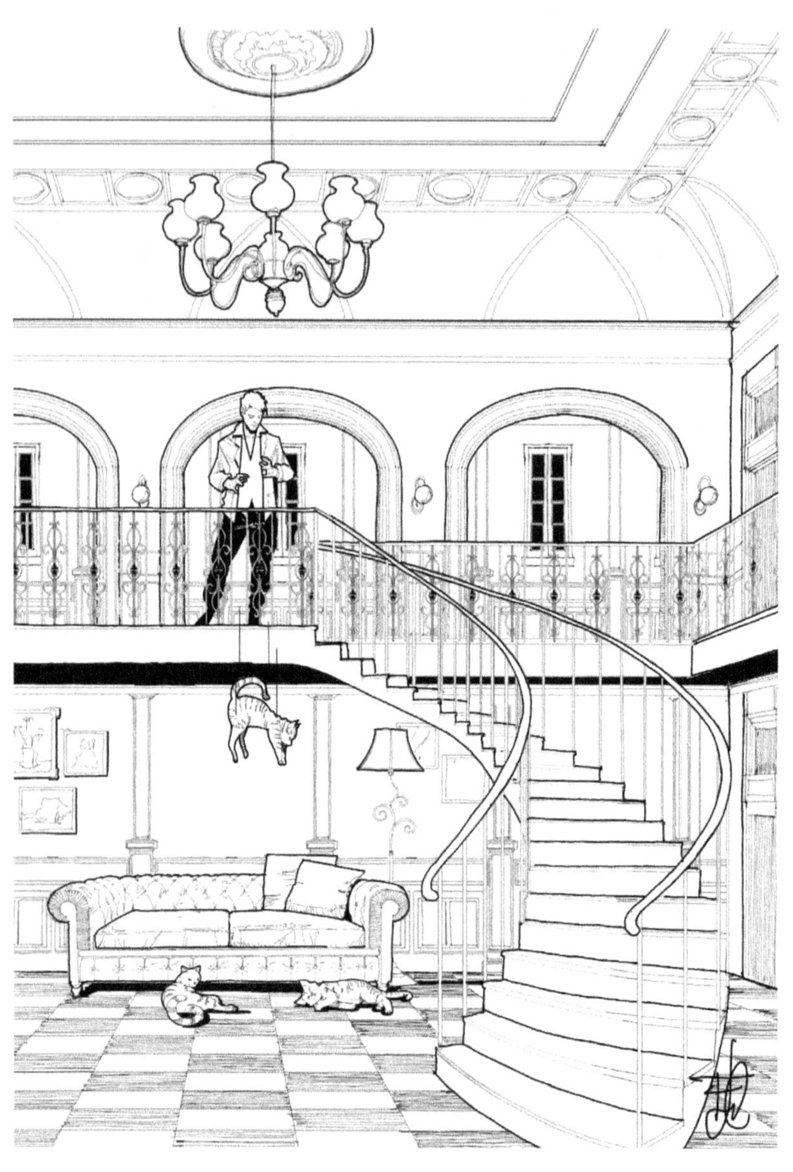

*Jerry held the cat over the edge
and dropped it neatly onto the small couch*

kat scratch fever

CHAPTER 1

"**GOOD NEWS, KAT,**" said Jerry, putting down his phone.

"Mmhm?" she replied, tapping her front teeth together to pause a novel scrolling on her Slimlines.

"That was my friend Colin. He's on his way over."

"Oh no," groaned Kat. "Isn't he the guy who pretends he's British?"

"The very same, but cut him some slack – it's all his crazy family's fault. They have pretentions of being one of the last bastions of British culture and they went and shipped him off in his youth to New Britannia and some pseudo-English boarding school. I think it ruined him for life, quite frankly, but he's still a stand-up guy. Putting up with the fake accent is a small price to pay."

Jerry and Kat were currently holed-up in a quiet seaside resort on the tropical planet Noom, contemplating their next moves. Kat wanted to push on toward the Ganymede constellation in search of a potential new world, but Jerry thought the Camelopardis galaxy held the best promise, since it boasted several stars very similar to Earth's Sol. Until they could resolve their difference of opinion they were staying put.

When it came right down to it, though, neither one was any too anxious to be moving on. They were getting lazy.

The door buzzed and Colin's beaming face filled the monitor screen.

"What, was he calling from the lobby?" asked Kat. "That's not a good sign, Jerry. This is no impromptu visit – he's got something in mind."

Jerry opened the door and Colin burst into the room, all smiles and back-slapping and *How-are-you-old-chaps*-ing and *Haven't-seen-you-in-ages*-ing and the like.

Once they finally settled down with drinks on the balcony overlooking the ocean, Colin's demeanour became a bit more sombre and, without further preamble, he said, "Say, Jerry, old bean, I'm in a frightful pickle and I'm hoping you can lend a hand, you know, be a pal and do me a solid, hmm?"

Without waiting for a response, he pushed on. He looked like nothing so much as a man wrestling with inner demons, with the demons favoured seven to three by those in the know.

"Now, I admit, to look at me one probably says to himself, 'Why that Colin's a lucky guy – has the world on a string, as it were. Surely he hasn't a care in the world. Life of Riley and all that rot.'

"But as so often is the case in this dashed human comedy we suffer within, the facts of the matter are much bleaker than would appear to the casual eye.

"And it's all my Aunt's Althea's fault."

"Your aunt? What has she got to do with your troubles?"

"Aunt Althea is the current Administrator of my family's finances and if you'd ever met her, Jerry, you'd say she reminds you of a classical sculpture of a Greek goddess."

"She's really that beautiful?" asked Jerry.

"No, I mean she's distant, rigid, and has a cold lump of stone for a heart."

Colin barked out a bitter laugh. He had about him the air of a man who has read an advance copy of his life story and wants to have a harsh word with the author.

"And if you knew what a pickle she's put me in, you'd say I was being charitable."

He took a long swallow from his glass. Obviously he was about to embark on a tale of woe which required a strengthening of fortitude.

"Jerry, I know this must come as a shock to you," – *which means*, thought Jerry, *that this won't come as a shock at all* – "but there's scarcely a civilised planet left where I dare show my face without risking being tarred and feathered by the local merchantry.

"You see, some time ago my vexatious relative irrationally got the notion into her head that my character would be improved by my suffering a bit of hardship. You know – 'forged in the furnace', what?

"And she determined that the best means to accomplish this rather dubious objective was to cut off my allowance. Left me without so much as a blasted penny."

"Wait," said Kat. "You still have an allowance? At your age?"

Colin drew himself up into a rigid posture, the better to peer down his nose at her. "Certainly I do. And age has nothing to do with it. This is my *birthright*.

"Evidently," he continued, shrinking once again into the shriveled husk of a man that the telling of this tale rendered him, "She expected me to…" he was having trouble wrenching the words from his lips, but with superhuman effort he finally said, "To get a… *job*."

As this last word passed his lips his body was wracked by a deep shudder, not unlike that of someone who has just noticed the corpse of a hairy black spider at the bottom of their now-empty coffee cup.

Out of deference to the gravity of this revelation the three sat quietly for a moment, staring at the waves crashing against the shore.

Finally, after a respectful silence, he continued.

"Of course, you can well guess what actually happened: ever since that tragic day I have been forced to hop from planet to planet, always one step ahead of the proverbial wolf at my door, racking up frightfully large debts in each venue before the true state of my financial affairs becomes known to the locals and I must perform a midnight dash.

"But I fear my golden goose has laid its last egg. Word is getting round. Why, at my last lodgings it wasn't more than three days before management slipped a decidedly snippy note underneath my door advising me that an advance payment would be required if I expected to continue laying down the old noggin on their pillows.

"Which brings me to you, Jerry, old pal."

Jerry eyed him carefully, similar to how one might react to the effusive greetings of a long-lost pal who works for a local charity and happens to cross one's path right at the time of the annual appeal.

"Hm-hm," responded Jerry noncommittally.

Credit Colin with at least the basic perspicacity to recognise a wary quarry.

"Now Jerry, don't look at me like I'm a hungry cheetah inviting an antelope with a sprained ankle over for drinks.

"I'm not here to put the touch on you. I've something far more… *visionary* in mind, and you're the perfect fellow for it.

"This whole nasty misadventure was the result of my aunt's misbegotten muliebral concept of character-building. And knowing her as I do, I guarantee you that neither Hell nor high water can alter her viewpoint. She is, to put it mildly, intractable.

"And she will never relent in her present course of action until she is proved right. And that is where you, my dear chum, can be of invaluable service to your humble servant who sits before you now, hat in hand, as it were."

"I can prove your aunt right?"

"Exactly! I'm delighted you've grasped the gist of it so readily.

"I intend to introduce you to my aunt as my present employer and mentor. You shall regale her with tales of my insightful business acumen, unswerving devotion to duty, the old nose to the grindstone thing, etc etc, and she shall be so completely bowled over by my miraculous transformation that the joy which greeted the return of the original Prodigal Son shall seem reserved in comparison. I daresay it won't be enough to slaughter merely just a fatted calf or two, she will insist on the whole herd."

"You want me to boast about your 'business acumen'."

"'Insightful'," clarified Colin.

"Your 'devotion to duty'."

"'Unswerving'," agreed Colin.

"And you expect me to do this when?"

"At the soonest, old bean. I shall invite you to the ancestral homestead this weekend and in the course of our time there you'll ingratiate yourself to the old blister so effectively that her stony heart will be miraculously transformed into a warm beating human organ, and I shall once again be welcomed into the fold with restored financial resources, and the means at my disposal to pay off the Visigoths before they begin storming the gates."

Jerry looked at Kat. They both shrugged.

Why not? It's not like our calendar is full.

"Oh, one last thing, old bean – I want you to bring along a dog. The old biddy's absolutely bonkers about animals. You can't help but get in solid with her if you cart along some beast. Tell her you can't bear to be separated, etc. Tug at the old heartstrings."

"I don't have a dog."

"I already anticipated that –" and so saying, Colin trotted over to the door and plucked up a basket that he had left lying in the foyer.

"I brought along my dog."

A small brown creature looked up from the basket, yawned, then jumped out and ran over to sniff at Jerry's feet.

"You see? He likes you already! His name is Trevor. Take care with him – I shouldn't be able to bear it if anything happened to the little fellow."

And promising to have a transport waiting for Jerry at the local station Friday morning, he was gone, merrily humming a showtune as he trotted off down the hallway.

"You know, this might be fun," said Kat, bending down to scratch behind the little dog's ears. "Colin's whole family is British and I do simply the best English accent! I'll fit in swell there –"

"Oh no you don't," said Jerry. "If you come along you'll put the kibosh on the whole thing. The invitation was for me alone. It's highly unlikely I'll be able to work my magic with the old bird if I've got you tagging along asking silly questions like, 'Have you ever met the Queen?'"

"But –"

"No 'buts'. You're not coming, that's final."

As pronouncements go, this merited inclusion in the list of Most Foolish Statements, right alongside quotes from the Captain of the Titanic and the guy from Decca records who declined to sign the Beatles.

Kat got a cold, hard look in her eyes that could have been plucked straight from Sisyphus as he prepared for yet another attempt up the hill. Jerry pretended not to notice.

CHAPTER II

LATER THAT EVENING, as Jerry and Kat lay relaxing on the balcony, he gazing at the stars and Kat looking at God Knows What on her Slimlines, Kat said, "Jerry, isn't Colin's last name 'Chudleigh'?

"Mm-hm," he replied quietly, wondering what she was up to now.

"And his family currently resides in a mock English country estate on the planet of Nottingham? Where you're going this weekend?"

"What's your point?"

"Well," said Kat meaningfully, "As it happens, it turns out our dear friend has an intimate connection to a rather nettlesome problem currently plaguing the scientific community."

Sigh.

"OK, spill it, Kat. But don't think anything you say can change my mind."

"Patience, grasshopper. Wait me out here.

"According to this article I'm reading, one dear departed Percy Chudleigh, MD, PhD, late of the garden planet of Nottingham, who met his premature demise four months ago while working in his lab at NovoHealth Inc., was inconsiderate enough to shuffle off this mortal coil without first having the courtesy to share with management his computer password.

"Now, I'm sure this sort of thing happens all the time and little notice is paid, but this particular instance is especially significant because it seems our Dr. P. Chudleigh had recently discovered the cure for Masslen's Syndrome."

This last bit of news got Jerry's attention.

Masslen's Syndrome was a blight on space travel. When ships were enveloped by the graviton bubble that transported them through space in multiples of light speeds, some humans experienced symptoms similar to altitude sickness – except in the case of Masslen's Syndrome, victims died within minutes.

Worst of all, there was nothing to predict who was susceptible, and in fact a person could travel once, dozens or even hundreds of times and then without warning, for no discernable reason, suddenly be stricken with an attack and die on the spot.

Masslen's Syndrome was the terror of every space-traveling individual. To find a cure was the Holy Grail.

And apparently Colin's relative had done exactly that.

"You're shitting me. How have I never heard about this before?"

"Because the good doctor expired before he could publish. And all his data and research is encrypted in his computer behind an impenetrable password."

"No such thing. Any good quantum computer – such as the one in your Slimlines – can crack any password in a matter of hours."

"Not this password. You can take my word on this one, Jerry. One thing Retrievers know is encryption – it's our stock in trade: a Discovery isn't worth dirt if you can't safeguard the critical details during your trip back to Earth.

"And according to the article I'm reading, the good doctor was an encryption nerd. He used asymmetric cryptography with a one-way 'trapdoor' function requiring two keys for decryption. I think he was planning on sending his research to his bosses and the scientific journals using a public-private key encryption. We have the 'public' key that he created. But in this particular instance we can't decode without the matching 'private' key."

"Again, quantum computer, cracked in hours, etc," said Jerry.

"Except his public key is 3 billion characters long. It's likely that the private key is of equal length. Even for a roomful of networked quantum computers, cracking a password that's three billion characters long would take centuries."

"How does anyone remember a password that's three billion characters long? Let alone type it in?"

"Now you're just being silly, Jer. You do neither thing – you store the password in some secret device that you can then use to upload the password into your system."

"Are we to assume that NovoHealth has searched the late doctor's lab right down to the molecular level looking for said key-storage device?"

"We are, but I am a believer in Fate. I think this opportunity has been dropped in our laps by the Universe for a reason. And that reason is to make us rich. Um, rich*er*."

"Don't be foolish, Kat. Even if we could somehow access the doctor's computer – which has no doubt been seized and locked away in the galaxy's most secure vault – and even if we could crack the uncrackable password, we still couldn't do anything with the research for the cure. It belongs to NovoHealth. They'd crush us like a bug if we tried to use their intellectual property."

"Well, yes, if we were trying to steal their property. But I'm not interested in that. I want them to develop a cure just as badly as you do. I'm interested in something else, something I see here in this article."

"Which is?"

"It's called a 'finder's fee', Jerry. NovoHealth has published the public key along with a sample encrypted file from the doctor's computer. They're offering a reward to anyone who can crack the encryption. No questions asked. Paid in cash."

"How much are they offering?" asked Jerry.

Jerry shouldn't have been taking a drink when she told him; they had to stop for a moment while he got a wad of napkins to clean up the mess.

"OK, Kat, you win," he sighed heavily. He understood how Napoleon must have felt when he got to Moscow.

"Tell me what you've got in mind."

THE DOCTOR'S LAB and local residence having already been scoured and found lacking in clues, Kat was convinced that the storage device must be secreted in the only remaining safe location – somewhere within his family's country estate manor.

Infiltrating NovoHealth's inter-office email system was child's play for Kat's Slimlines, and she learned that investigators from the NovoHealth corporation had visited the estate on Nottingham, but owing to the fact that the good doctor hadn't been there anytime in the last year and hadn't mailed anything there either, their inspection had been cursory, at best.

On the occasion of their visit the investigators had taken the opportunity to return to his family Dr. Chudleigh's few personal belongings from his lab. There wasn't much. They were:

One (1) cactus plant, origin Earth. Plant, soil and pot thoroughly searched, of course.

One (1) personal calendar, with various dates circled. All the dates, names and numbers had been closely examined; none had provided any discernable clues.

One (1) cat. Not purebred. Wearing a pink collar with little fishes embroidered on it. Collar was scanned, dissected and examined under an electron microscope. Nothing found. Cat was scanned as well, and thankfully not dissected. No electronic devices embedded anywhere on the animal.

Two (2) small photographs in lucite frames, one of the Queen and one of Dr. Chudleigh and his cat. Pictures scanned for microdots; nothing found.

There was nothing else.

"Jerry, we might not be able to find the storage device our good doctor was using at his lab, but I'll bet the last time he visited his family's estate he hid a backup device. I know those old country manors – the builders loved hiding secret rooms in them.

"And I'll bet you if we find a secret room, we'll find the storage device."

"And how do you propose we secretly search a huge country manor in one weekend without getting caught and tossed out on our ears?"

"My Slimlines can do it – with echolocation. All I have to do is to walk down each hallway looking to left and right, and any extra space that doesn't show up on the official blueprints will be our target. It's child's play!"

"Hm, you know, that doesn't sound like a bad plan. Did you pull a copy of the blueprints from the local county office?"

Grimacing, Kat shook her head. "Sadly, that's a big N-O, my dear. No such repository exists."

"Well that puts a bit of a kink into things, doesn't it?"

"Maybe not. It's a stone-by-stone recreation of the real Chudleigh manor back on Earth, and the architects who did this reproduction would have used 3-D mapping and replicated the original home right down to the last bit of mortar. There should be a copy of their 3-D scans and the new blueprints stored on one of the computers in the house.

"The problem is, I can't access any of the house's computers through the net. They're probably set up for in-person access only. We'll have to actually be onsite."

"I get that, Kat. You can come. But we still can't go together. You'll have to find a way to infiltrate the estate on your own."

Her wicked grin twigged him that she was already well ahead of him on this.

"According to a news article I found on the county website

entitled, 'Local Organization Offers A Helping Hand', Lady Chudleigh is on the Board of the township's 'Young Entrepreneurs Club'.

"About an hour ago I sent her social secretary an email requesting that she add to her kitchen staff an aspiring apprentice cook – a young lady who shows loads of promise and just needs a helping hand with her career. Happy to work for free, of course.

"A few minutes ago I received a reply. They want me to start next Monday morning.

"But I think I'll be getting there a few days early."

CHAPTER IV

THE LARGE MANOR grew more impressive the closer Jerry got; it was an ostentatious affair of two imposing storeys. Vines, rose bushes and several other species of plant that Jerry didn't recognise decorated the front of the house, providing a verdant backdrop to the numerous flowerbeds between it and a sweeping driveway encircling a huge decorative fountain.

The transport slid to a stop in front of a gigantic portico supported by classical Greek columns that sheltered two huge front doors from the elements.

Jerry climbed out of the little car and extracted his valise and the dog basket, placed Trevor on the ground, then turned and walked up the wide set of marble stairs and through the portico, the little dog following at his heels. Pressing his finger to an ornate button in the shape of a sunburst, he listened as a deep, rolling sound of bells rang out and echoed through the interior of the house.

Within about a moment, the door silently swung open to reveal a large distinguished-looking man, impeccably dressed in a perfectly pressed suit complete with tie and waistcoat.

The butler couldn't have been more than a couple of inches taller than Jerry, but his rigid posture and imposing carriage made Jerry feel like the man was virtually towering over him.

The servant did absolutely nothing to disabuse Jerry of this sensation, and in fact probably added to it by staring down the bridge of his nose at him.

"Hello, my good man," said Jerry, trying to inject a note of cheer and bonhomie into his greeting.

The butler looked at him wordlessly.

"Ah, I believe I'm expected," continued Jerry, discerning that further information needed to be forthcoming before the man would respond.

"I'm Colin's guest…" he added, hopefully.

This last nugget must have ticked the necessary box in the butler's mental checklist, for he replied, "Indeed, Sir. Please come in," and he turned and walked through the vestibule with Jerry on his heels. The door swung shut behind Jerry and closed with a quiet click.

They came into a huge atrium with sweeping circular stairways wrapping the walls on both sides. Wide doorways at various places along the walls indicated the presence of several large rooms situated to either side. A hallway at the opposite end led off into the interior of the house.

The butler paused and turned to Jerry, and asked, "Do you prefer accommodations on the east or the west side, Sir?"

"Oh, doesn't matter to me," said Jerry.

Notwithstanding his incredible discipline of demeanour, the butler couldn't help but wrinkle his nose ever so slightly as he spotted for the first time the small creature now sitting at Jerry's ankle.

"You have a *dog*, Sir," said the butler, choosing to point out the obvious and stressing the word "dog" with an emphasis that would normally be reserved for referring to a deadly plague sweeping through a city.

"Ah, yes, travels with me wherever I go. Constant companion and all that, you know."

"Indeed, Sir. Were you aware that this is primarily a *cat*-based domicile?"

Cats!

Jerry suddenly wanted to wring Colin's neck.

Why in God's Name did that moron suggest he bring a dog to a house with cats in it?

"Ah, no, I hadn't been apprised of that fact until just this moment, now that you mention it. But I can assure you that he has no bone to pick with any non-canine creatures – he's really the sweetest little guy…."

He reflexively looked down again at the dog, only to be met with the sight of an empty space beside his ankle. Panicking, he turned and looked behind him, then off to both sides, and was greeted by beautiful vistas of the elegant house, all impeccably dog-free.

The butler took no notice of the fact that their group was now missing one of its members, keeping Jerry firmly within the grip of his steely grey eyes and waiting patiently for him to cease his gyrations.

"Indeed, Sir. I will inform Lady Chudleigh. She likes to be kept apprised of all visitors to her home, especially those bearing four legs."

"Excellent!" replied Jerry with renewed enthusiasm.

"When can I meet the old bird?"

The butler's appearance became even more frosty as he icily replied, "*Lady* Chudleigh is presently otherwise occupied. I will inform her of your arrival at the earliest opportunity."

"And now, if you would be so kind as to follow me, I shall show you to your room, Sir," and so saying he turned and proceeded to the stairway sweeping up the right side of the atrium.

"Trevor!" Jerry hissed out in a forceful stage whisper, praying that bringing the little dog hadn't been a huge mistake.

The butler turned around.

"Sir?" he said quizzically.

Jerry looked at him with exasperation and said, "Nothing. I'm good. Thanks."

The butler, who had apparently also staked his own claim on a healthy supply of exasperation, quietly replied, "Quite so, Sir," and turned once again away from Jerry.

That damned dog was still nowhere in sight. Terrified what havoc the dumb beast might be about to unleash, Jerry called out again, softly but with painful urgency, *"TREVOR!"*

The shoulders on the butler's retreating form visibly slumped as he reluctantly came to a stop, even more reluctantly turned around to face Jerry, and with superhuman effort managed to replace the grimace on his face with an expression of at least slightly less hostility than he obviously wrestled with deep in his soul.

"Sir?" he replied levelly.

"For God's sake, I told you I'm fine," said Jerry, dumbfounded that this man couldn't seem to bear to tear himself away from him. *This must be what they mean by the attentive manservant,* thought Jerry. *But the fellow's carrying it just a bit too far.*

"Perhaps then, Sir, you might refrain from calling me back, if that would be acceptable," suggested the butler.

"What in the world makes you think I'm calling you?" asked Jerry.

"Well, Sir, that impression might stem from the fact that you keep calling my name."

"*Your* name's Trevor?" asked Jerry incredulously.

"Indeed, Sir."

"But that's my dog's name, too!"

"Your *dog* is named 'Trevor'?" asked the butler. He seemed offended even to consider the possibility.

"Indeed," replied Jerry.

Just at that moment the little beast came trotting up, having concluded his unknown excursion. Jerry wasted no time in scooping him up and heading up the stairs, the wounded-looking butler trailing in his wake.

As Jerry and the butler, who had regained his presence of mind, swept briskly up the stairs Jerry eyed the space below.

For the first time, he noted the attendance of several feline residents. They were everywhere, now that he looked closely.

Cats were curled up sleeping on various armchairs along the perimeter; there were two cats ensconced beneath a settee, one deep in dreamless slumber and the other meditatively chewing on a paw; there were two laying splayed out on a Persian carpet in a sitting room that Jerry spied off to the side, as well as a transient who was wandering through the scene from a side passageway.

"Just how many cats are there in this house?" Jerry asked the butler's back.

"One has long since lost count, I'm afraid, Sir," came the reply, as they arrived at the top of the stairs and the butler turned to conduct Jerry down a hallway that ran toward the back of the manor.

CHAPTER V

HE BUTLER LED Jerry to a small room after advising him that lunch would be served at noon, and then retreated back to his stronghold on the main floor. Jerry scanned the room unenthusiastically.

Hardly first-class accommodations, he thought.

A small shape on the bed stirred slightly, catching Jerry's attention. On closer inspection it revealed itself to be a sleeping tan-coloured cat.

Gingerly picking up the animal, Jerry carried it out to the hallway and over to the railing above the atrium. Spying the settee conveniently located almost directly below, he held the cat over the edge and dropped it neatly onto the small couch. It landed with a small plop.

Among those known for their passionate defense of their dominion, few can compare with the fierce Waorani tribe of the Ecuadorian Amazon, who have been known to issue statements such as "Anyone who enters our territory to destroy it must be killed". It is undeniable, however, that even these ferocious warriors are mere pushovers next to your average housecat.

At the sound of the little tan cat landing on the settee, the two cats beneath it, who had until that moment been pleasantly occupied with chewing their paws and surveying their realm with smug satisfaction, craned their necks out from under the settee to investigate the source of the puzzling sound they had just heard.

Dumbfounded to discover this interloper upon their domain,

mysteriously appearing seemingly out of thin air, they immediately concluded that this violation of their territorial prerogatives must not pass unchallenged.

They responded as can only be expected in such circumstances, by issuing forth two ear-splitting soprano yowls of feline outrage, which in turn elicited a similar response from the hapless tan cat, who, one must admit, was no more than an innocent pawn in this incursion upon their territory.

Notwithstanding the failure of their auricular assault to make any appreciable progress in resolving the feline Mexican standoff, the three screaming cats decided that the most effective strategy to employ in this encounter was to increase the intensity of their howls, which they did at greater and greater volumes that penetrated throughout the entire manor, each shriek building upon the other in a frenzied bid to bludgeon their adversary into submission purely with sound waves.

Of course, eventually someone had to blink, and the tan cat, concluding that a judicious retreat was now the most advisable course of action, suddenly leapt off the settee and made a frantic break for the hallway running towards the back of the house. The two other cats, savouring their moral victory and still intent on exacting redress, rapidly followed closely on his heels, all three continuing to shriek loudly as they scrambled away through the atrium and down the hallway, disappearing into the bowels of the house, their screams gradually fading away into the distance.

The sudden departure of the three cats from the atrium was mitigated by the arrival of several alarmed humans, as various guests, housemaids, and assorted other staff came running into the atrium in search of the feline slaughter which was evidently taking place, and all of whom, in the wake of the cats' hasty exodus, immediately turned their attention to Jerry, who unwisely still stood looking over the railing above the cats' recent field of battle.

One of the younger housemaids who had been mopping the floor on the far side of the atrium called out (impertinently, in Jerry's opinion), "Oi! Are you throwing cats off the balcony?"

"Throw? Cats?" babbled Jerry. "No! No no no no no no no, I didn't throw him… that is – "

His voice trailed off as he immediately discerned that any protestations of his innocence, no matter how vehement, were pointless.

The butler and the senior housekeeper exchanged knowing glances. The housemaids exchanged knowing glances. The other guests exchanged knowing glances. The remaining cats in the room exchanged knowing glances. Noah building his Ark, had he been present on the scene, would have immediately recognised in Jerry a kindred soul.

Muttering quietly among themselves, Jerry's audience gradually disbanded, leaving Jerry grinning sheepishly at the butler, who was the last remaining on the scene. Eventually, seeing no additional beasts writhing within Jerry's grasp, he reluctantly concluded it was safe to withdraw once again to his butlery refuge.

Jerry sighed heavily, then returned to his room and unpacked his valise.

Sitting on the bed, he took a deep breath and thought, *Well, no time like the present. Might as well go hunt down that computer.*

Quietly, he slipped out of his room and down the stairs. He was pleased to see that the maids had all dispersed, and he gingerly approached the hallway leading to the back of the house. He felt it most likely that the computer would not be situated in one of the large front rooms, but rather somewhere a bit more private.

Heading down the hallway, he tried several doors but to his chagrin found them locked. He was about to turn and try the doors on the other side of the hallway when he noticed that the door farthest down was slightly ajar.

Jerry gingerly stepped inside the room and squinted into the dim interior. He appeared to be in Lady Chudleigh's office. And at the far end of the room, on an ornate wooden desk, sat a computer!

Never one to look a gift horse in the mouth, Jerry quietly clicked shut the door behind himself and hustled over to the desk. A small ginger cat with a white dot on the middle of its forehead lay sleeping on the desk.

Rolling his eyes, Jerry picked up the cat and unceremoniously dropped it onto the floor. Then, tapping the screen, he grimaced to see a password box pop up.

He had expected as much, of course. He had brought a remote transmitter that would connect the computer with Kat's Slimlines, but he was annoyed to have to wait for her arrival before he could access the files. At least he'd found the computer, though.

Just then, his attention was drawn to the room's sliding French doors that led onto the patio and the west gardens. The door was making a scratching sound.

No, thought Jerry. *Not the door.* The noise was being generated by the cat which he had removed from the desk, who was now scratching to get out.

"Here you go, kitty," said Jerry softly, as he unlatched the door and opened it slightly.

As soon as the door was opened the cat bolted out and onto the patio, and Jerry slid the door shut. He quickly hustled over to the door to the hallway, silently pulled it open and slipped back out of the room. And came face to face with a downstairs maid holding a rag and a bottle of furniture polish.

"Oh! Begging your pardon, Sir, I was just polishing up the furniture. I had to go get more polish. Were you looking for Lady Chudleigh?"

"Ah, no no, that's OK, I was just looking for the… bathroom."

"That would be closer to the front of the house, Sir. The door that's marked with a little floral tile that says 'WC'."

"Oh, I saw that. I thought it meant… 'Winter Clothes'. You know, a clothes closet."

Before the maid could respond to this admittedly pathetic response, Jerry was off up the hallway, then disappeared into one of the larger rooms off the atrium.

CHAPTER VI

THE ROOM THAT Jerry escaped into was the library, a large, airy brightly lit space with numerous couches and armchairs, all encircled by walls covered in bookshelves groaning with books.

Hearing a small sound behind him he turned and saw that Trevor – the dog, not the butler – had followed him downstairs and was now sniffing around the room.

Jerry walked over to the wide French doors overlooking the house's extensive patio and west gardens and tried to pull them open but they were locked shut. He was about to unlatch them when he heard a soft cough behind him.

Trevor – the butler, not the dog – was standing at the room's entrance.

"May I present Lady Chudleigh, Sir," he intoned.

He stepped aside to reveal an imperious looking woman in severe clothing who carried a lorgnette in her left hand, through which she was now peering at Jerry.

Jerry walked over quickly and offered his hand.

"Lady Chudleigh, it's a pleasure."

"For me as well, Mr. –"

Now, Jerry had determined that his efforts to ingratiate himself with the Lady Chudleigh would be aided by adopting a British heritage of his own, and had decided to employ an alias for his weekend sojourn.

During the trip over from the station he had run through a series of typical English names, eliminating them one by one as too famous (Churchill) or too cliché (Windsor) or too difficult to spell (Postlethwaite). Finally he had settled on one which was obviously British, but not too common, and easy to spell.

"Cromwell," he said, with a pleasant smile.

The old lady visibly stiffened, and might even have withdrawn her proffered hand had it not been for her impeccable sense of etiquette.

"*'Cromwell',*" she repeated. "As in the *traitor* Oliver Cromwell?" she asked icily.

Jerry immediately regretted his admitted weakness in the specifics of English history, and reflected that perhaps he should have applied a bit more research into the names he was considering.

"Ah, well, some might also say 'patriot', you know..." he stammered, hoping that the man's deeds might be open to alternative interpretations. "Two sides to every coin, what?"

"If you consider deposing the reigning monarch and setting yourself up in his place a 'patriotic act', then you may have a point. Is that your position, Mr." – *shudder* – "Cromwell?"

"Ah, no, I'm a monarchist along with the best of them – 'the king is dead, long live the king', what what?"

To Jerry's dismay, there was no understanding smile evoked by his remarks.

And then the old lady looked down at Jerry's ankle where the small dog sat looking up expectantly and wagging his tail. She wrinkled her nose as she peered down at the beast, then raised her eyes back up to meet Jerry's and, replete with significance, carefully said, "We have *cats* in this house."

Inwardly, Jerry sighed. He hoped this wasn't going to become a frequent refrain among those he encountered. He did his best to assemble on his face what he hoped would pass for a reassuring smile, filled with warmth and love for all mankind, evoking images of cherubs frolicking gaily in flower-covered meadows.

"Ah, no problem. Little Trevor here loves cats. Some of his best friends are cats, heh heh. Cats won't be a problem."

The old lady seemed unconvinced.

"Your dog's name is 'Trevor'?"

"Ah," he stammered, and added by way of explanation, "My father's name was Trevor…."

The old lady looked at Jerry with a pathetic expression of abject pity and said, "I'm sure he is very proud."

"Oh, that's alright," replied Jerry casually. "He's dead."

Silence descended as a heavy veil settling over the scene. The old lady, ruminating on his revelation, peered closely at Jerry through her lorgnette.

"I should like to continue this conversation, Mr. Cromwell," she said after a moment. "I have something to attend to at the moment, but perhaps you could join me in the conservatory for some tea in a half hour."

Jerry's enthusiastic agreement was met with a simple nod and the old lady turned and walked away.

WAITING OUT THE thirty minutes, Jerry wandered down the long hallway that stretched off to the back of the house.

Along both sides of the hallway were mounted huge paintings in ornate frames depicting various classical events. Each frame bore a small brass plaque at its base describing the scene.

Having been an avid classical scholar in his youth, Jerry recognised almost all the tableaux and walked down the hallway closely inspecting each, especially the portrayals of great battles and famous mythological figures. He thoughtfully examined an illustration of Alexander astride a great black stallion at the Battle of the Persian Gate, and one of the Greek god Hades carrying off Persephone to the Underworld, and finally one he didn't know, of a woman with a cat head.

He squinted down at the brass plaque which read,

Sekhmet, a warrior goddess in Egyptian mythology with the head of a lioness

Huh, he thought. *The old biddy has some diverse tastes.*

Suddenly sensing a presence behind him, Jerry spun around, expecting to find that Trevor – the butler, not the dog – had once again silently sidled up behind him.

There was no one there, though, and Jerry was about to turn back around when a hint of movement caught his eye. Looking down, he noticed that a cat was strolling along the hallway.

The cat, having no doubt ascertained that Jerry held nothing edible, calmly walked on by and disappeared into a door through a cat flap, a feature which Jerry now noticed every door included.

But this door seemed to be especially popular. During the next few minutes Jerry watched as several cats strolled over to the door from various directions and disappeared inside. Curiosity piqued, Jerry walked over to the door and tried the handle. It was locked.

And then Jerry noticed something strange. The air around the door felt cold. He pressed his hand against the door and was surprised to note that it felt several degrees cooler than the rest of the house.

He looked down at the cat flap and noticed that it was swaying slightly inwards. Getting down on his hands and knees and lowering his ear to the cat door, he was able to hear a soft whisper of air being sucked into the room past the edges of the flap.

As he crouched on all fours, inclining his head against the cat door and listening intently for any telltale sounds from within, he spied to his left two very large shoes just inches from his face, surmounted by the hem of two perfectly pressed grey gabardine trouser legs.

He tilted his head further and followed the expanse of trouser legs up until his view ended with the sight of a face towering far above them, a face which was intently peering down at him.

Quickly scrambling to his feet Jerry sheepishly grinned at the butler, who deployed a gaze at him that would have had Medusa weeping in envy.

"Ah… I saw a cat go through here…" stammered Jerry. "I thought it might be in trouble…."

"'In trouble'," repeated the butler.

"Yes, ah, I was worried…."

Just at that moment a small noise came from the cat flap as a cat stepped out and, taking no note of either man, calmly walked away down the hall.

"Let us all breathe a sigh of relief," said the butler dryly. "The crisis has passed."

"Lady Chudleigh will see you now," he said. "If you feel there are no additional feline emergencies which demand your intervention, please follow me."

AS JERRY ENTERED the conservatory he was immediately seized by the impression he had taken a wrong turn somehow and had stumbled into a wildlife habitat.

The door opened onto a large, glass-walled sun house. Obscured within a jungle of huge potted tropical plants, palm, citrus and banana trees and miscellaneous flowering exotics, were a multitude of parrots and similar colourful birds in spacious birdcages, interspersed liberally with wicker couches, settees, and various armchairs, each of which boasted at least one cat.

The cats definitely outnumbered the birds, who warily eyed their feline roommates with suspicion from within their barred sanctuaries. It seemed to Jerry to be a bestial reenactment of the siege of the German army by the Russians at Stalingrad. With the obvious difference being, of course, that the Russians didn't want to actually *eat* the German soldiers.

For their part, the cats, as cats are wont to do, exhibited a general demeanour of haughty disinterest in their surroundings, occupying themselves with such essential cat pastimes as chewing on their paws, licking various and sundry body parts, and – of course – sleeping.

It was through this herbaceous menagerie landscape, feeling like Stanley in the African jungle searching for Livingstone, that Jerry picked his way over to the settee where Lady Chudleigh sat meditatively applying needlework while a large fat Persian cat slept beside her on a red velvet pillow embroidered with the name "Augustus".

On a chair closest to where she was sitting reclined a sleek tan cat, which Jerry recognised as the cat which he had earlier removed from his room. The cat was sleeping peacefully, and there remained no sign of the intra-species tensions which had sadly marred the cat's previous interaction with his feline brethren. Apparently, in the world of cats, all is easily forgotten and forgiven.

He approached the old woman and stood expectantly before her chair, but she took no note of his arrival and did not look up from her needlework.

As he stood there, Jerry considered that perhaps he should perform for the old matriarch like a court jester, and he was torn between breaking into a stirring rendition of "My Old Kentucky Home" or a spirited performance of "Camptown Racetrack".

It was not a decision to be made lightly, reflected Jerry, for while the former was excellently suited to showing off his superb baritone voice, the latter definitely held the upper hand in its opportunity to showcase his soft-shoe footwork skills, which he considered so impressive that he was sure that even Mr. Bojangles, were he to witness it, would have been signing up for dance lessons before the number was over.

Before he could make his decision, however, Lady Chudleigh finally acknowledged Jerry's presence.

"Won't you sit down, Mr. Cromwell," she said, still barely deigning to glance up from her needlework.

"May I offer you a spot of tea?"

Jerry, declining the tea, gingerly lifted the tan cat from the armchair and gently deposited the loudly complaining animal on the floor, before setting himself down in its former place in the chair next to the old lady.

"My nephew tells me you are his employer, although," and here she squinted intently through her pince-nez at Jerry as a taxidermist might size up a carcass, "You appear to be a bit younger than I would have thought.

"Still," she continued, in a tone rife with significance, "You never can tell these days. So many people have prioritized youthful appearance above mature behaviour."

Jerry had no response. Her comment, it seemed to him, qualified excellently as a non-sequitur.

The old basilisk continued unabated.

"It's usually not until a man settles down and has children that he develops any true semblance of maturity.

"Do you have any children, Mr. Cromwell?"

This last query did not take Jerry by surprise. He had already formulated in his mind a well fleshed-out backstory of devoted family man and strict father figure.

"Why, yes," he replied. "I have a boy and a girl."

"How nice," responded Lady Chudleigh, and then pitched an unexpected curve ball at Jerry, who despite his best efforts to construct an admirable persona had neglected to fill in the details.

"What are their names?"

With the almost infinite variety of human names to choose from, one would have assumed that Jerry could field this high lob with ease, but somehow, as is so often the case when spinning a web of lies, his mind went completely blank and the first two names that came out of his lips were appellations that he had most recently seen on the little brass plates on the picture frames in the hallway.

"Ah, Bucephalus and Persephone."

This revelation at least provided the effect of momentarily pausing the old lady's work on her needlepoint.

"I must say, those are decidedly unusual names to give modern children. How did you come to choose them?"

"Ah, no method really…. Just picked them at random, I suppose."

It could have been worse, he thought. *At least I didn't say "Sekmet".*

"So if I am to understand you, Mr. Cromwell, your dear departed father you honour by naming your dog after him, but your children's names you picked randomly, as out of a hat."

"Well, I blame their mother," replied Jerry.

Jerry developed the distinct impression that the interview was rapidly going off the rails and he made a desperate attempt to haul it back from the edge.

"And you, Lady Chudleigh? Is there a Lord Chudleigh skulking about the grounds somewhere, heh heh?"

"I am sad to report that my soul mate passed on several years ago."

"Oh, I'm so sorry to hear that," mumbled Jerry.

"It's quite alright – he had a wonderful peaceful passing. I held him in my arms and kissed him."

So it was murder, thought Jerry.

"Thirty wonderful years of wedded bliss we shared together. We met fairly late in life, but it was love at first sight."

That must have been a pretty dark room.

As the old dowager briefly paused to sip at her tea, Jerry's eye happened to fall on a little black & white cat wandering through the room. His meanderings took him in proximity to each of the various cats distributed throughout the room, who would then look down grumpily at the interloper and quietly hiss; the little cat would then move on a few feet and meet up with the next resident, and the sequence would repeat.

"That little guy seems to be cattus non gratus," observed Jerry wittily (he hoped). *Perhaps discussing the cats will put the old crone in a better mood.*

Lady Chudleigh regarded the black & white cat with obvious disdain. "That nasty mongrel," was all she said.

Well, that went well, thought Jerry. *Maybe a different tack….*

A gardener was working quietly at the far end of the sunroom, and his presence inspired Jerry.

"You have a wonderful home, Lady Chudleigh," he offered, hoping not to sound too obsequious. "You must employ a frightful number of servants."

The old lady responded with what can only be characterized as a "snort".

"Ha! Not quite as many as in recent days, I should say."

She leaned toward Jerry and in conspiratorial tones revealed, "A few days ago I happened to come downstairs in the late evening for a spot of tea. Normally I would have rung for it, but the urge to exercise my legs motivated me to visit the kitchen in person.

"You might imagine my shock when on my approach I overheard a number of the staff conversing at their evening table.

"They were *mocking our home and the village,* Mr. Cromwell, using an offensive caricature of our British speech!

"I will tolerate many offenses, but I refuse to endure scorn heaped upon British culture.

"I fired the lot, on the spot. Gave them one hour to be off the premises. And I have instructed Trevor to sack any other similarly impudent individual who finds it amusing to deride our English heritage by parodying our speech."

A remote part of Jerry's brain seemed to discern this nugget of information as somehow valuable, but at the moment the majority of his cerebral functions were focused on the cat which had come to sit on his foot.

He recognised it as the feline whom he had displaced. The cat, reluctant to abandon its territory, had chosen to settle down on Jerry's shoe and to amuse itself with batting around the laces.

Just then the door to the main house opened and Trevor (butler) stepped into the sunroom, checking to ensure that his mistress had not been strangled or chopped into small pieces and buried in the plants. He softly closed the door behind himself and discreetly assessed the scene.

He didn't notice that immediately behind him Trevor (dog) had slipped through the cat flap and – inadvisedly, in Jerry's opinion – entered the room and begun to sniff around.

If there's one event that's guaranteed to snag the attention of a gaggle of cats, the introduction of a dog into the scene is it. Immediately every cat in the room, instantly alert, puffed up to twice its normal size as though a gigantic cloud of static electricity had descended on the lot. A soft sibilation of hissing filled the chamber.

Blissfully unaware, the canine Daniel, tail happily wagging, began blithely strolling through the now-energized lion's den.

Eventually, the little dog's meanderings inevitably led him into close proximity with an especially puffed, vigourously hissing resident.

Future historians will heatedly debate the exact sequence of the events which next transpired, but the advantage will surely lie with those who focus on the injudicious rendezvous between the dog and his puffy adversary.

No doubt heeding the advice of generations of ancestors passed down through his DNA, the cat employed the age-old, tried-and-tested feline greeting which has served so many members of its species so well.

With one lightning stroke, he reached out and sliced a magnificent gash across the little dog's nose.

The reaction, as one might expect, was immediate and breathtaking.

Never would Jerry have predicted that an animal as small as the little dog could scream at the volume he produced. Jerry counted it lucky that the glass walls of the conservatory did not shatter at the ear-splitting shriek that issued forth from the hapless canine. And which, in turn, set off all the birds in the room, who immediately broke into piercing shrieks and screeching danger calls, flapping their wings and rattling their cages.

Further, it is an undeniable truth that, once on alert, a cat needs little provocation to lapse into panic. At the sound of the dog's wail and the birds' shrieks every cat in the room, already on edge, rocketed into action, springing from chairs and tables and shelves, scrambling and skidding and skittering out of control on the slick tile floor, knocking over lamps and vases and various small potted plants, exploding in a frenzied mass rush for the exit.

As luck would have it, the cat which had thus far been satisfied with the harmless amusement of batting around Jerry's shoelaces had evidently decided his days performing on the Amateur Circuit were complete and he was now ready to go Professional. And it was at the exact moment of the dog's unfortunate interaction that he chose to sink his claws as deeply as they could go into Jerry's ankle.

"SON OF A —" Jerry howled, and kicked his foot out and away from the pitchfork which had just impaled it.

Had there been in attendance a group of scouts for the Premier Soccer Leagues, no doubt a heated bidding war for Jerry's services would have erupted on the spot, as the speed and strength of his kick was a wonder to behold.

The sanguinary feline, which had maintained the incautious policy of perching on Jerry's shoe throughout its assault, was consequently launched through the air at the speed of a supersonic missile.

No doubt you have seen the promotional videos for the circus where the strong man allows himself to be shot in the chest by a cannonball. He clutches the projectile as it impacts his form and magnificently staggers back a step or two as he absorbs the blow.

Thus was the scene as the airborne cat rocketed across the room and collided squarely with the butler's sternum.

Shortsightedly not having anticipated an assault with ballistic cats, the butler was taken unawares and upon impact stumbled back two or three steps, each footfall eliciting screeching shrieks as he trod heavily upon various cats' tails or feet as the maelstrom of panicked felines convulsed around his ankles in their frenzied dash for the cat door.

Within no more than ten to fifteen seconds, the conservatory was completely cat-free.

The birds all stopped screeching. The dog silently cowered in terror beneath a settee. The receding rapid click-clack of cat claws skittering away down the hallway gradually dwindled to nothing.

The silence that then descended upon the room was punctuated only by the quiet swishing of the cat flap in the door as it settled to a stop, and by the various drips, tinkles and wobbling sounds left in the wake of the feline stampede.

The magnificent red velvet pillow – now vacant – that lay beside Lady Chudleigh displayed two long tremendous gashes where its recent occupant had employed its claws to enable a faster takeoff.

One by one, the butler gently plucked each of the tan cat's claws from off his waistcoat where the stunned beast still adhered to him like ivy on a brick wall, as it had evidently determined that clinging to the butler's sternum was the safest position in which to weather the recent feline storm.

One of the parrots, in a futile attempt to defuse the uncomfortable tension that had settled over the room, loudly invited one and all to join him in partaking of a delicious nut.

Jerry cleared his throat.

Lifting his arm, he pointedly extended his wrist and looked at his watch.

"My goodness," he said. "Look how late it's gotten. I must be off to change for lunch."

And without another word he scooped up the whimpering little dog from under the settee and, detouring slightly to avoid the now-cat-free butler, exited the room.

Y GOODNESS, TREVOR," whispered the old lady, sitting shell-shocked in the eerie quiet of the post-apocalyptic conservatory. "Whatever do you make of that fellow?"

The butler, as a rule disinclined to voice his opinions of the household's guests, coughed diplomatically.

"I fear that there may be…." He briefly pondered how to put into words his assessment that Jerry was quite mad, and that all their lives were probably in danger from the distinct possibility that their deranged houseguest would imminently be sent over the edge by an ordinarily trivial matter, such as a bowl of soup with too much seasoning, or perhaps an overstarched bedsheet, said event jostling loose once and for all the man's tenuous grip on sanity and compelling him to murder them all in their beds while they slept.

"I fear there may be… something amiss… upstairs," he said, illustrating his point by tapping meaningfully against his temple with his forefinger.

Unfortunately, the old lady, still somewhat discombobulated by the recent feline cataclysm, was peering down intently at her needlework and completely missed the all-important visual cue, and consequently misunderstood the normally discreet butler's comment.

"Something wrong upstairs? You mean there's a problem with his room? Well that won't do, Trevor, that won't do at all. We have *standards* in this house, no matter the quality of the guest! Move him at once to another room!"

"Madam, I fear that you may have misunder—"

"Not another word about the matter, Trevor! I won't have this household's reputation sullied by careless treatment of a guest – move him immediately, I say."

Sigh.

"As you wish, madam."

CHAPTER X

JERRY HUSTLED OUT of the conservatory with the little dog under his arm and made a beeline to the nearest exit he could find to the west gardens.

"Here," said Jerry unhappily, dropping the dog on the ground. "Go chase some squirrels or something." And he sunk down onto a small bench and morosely gazed out. That hadn't gone anywhere nearly as well as he had hoped it would, he reflected.

"Oi!" came a call from his left.

He looked to see a gardener hustling over to him.

"I wouldn't let the little fellow do that if I were you, Sir," he said, pointing to the dog which was now snuffling around in a small pile of leaves. "There's venomous snakes out at this time of year on this planet."

Seeing Jerry's startled expression, he said, "Oh, it's nothing for you or me to worry about, Sir – they're plumb terrified of humans, won't come anywhere near us. But the animals, that's a different matter. We keep all the pets indoors this season. It'll all be OK in a month or two when the baby snakes have all grown up and learned to hide, but for now if you want to let him out to do his business you should wait until evening when the snakes have gone back down into their holes, or keep to the horse pastures on the east side. There's no snakes there."

Thanking the gardener, Jerry trotted over and scooped up Trevor and carried him over to the horse pastures, where he leaned on a rail meditatively while the dog ran around in the grass and chased butterflies.

Eventually the little beast tired of his exertions and came back, wagging his tail. Jerry picked him up and reentered the house by the same doors he had used to exit.

On his way to the stairway he was met by the butler, who stopped him to announce, "Lady Chudleigh has requested that we move you to more spacious accommodations, Sir. I have taken the liberty of moving your belongings to your new room farther down the hall."

That's odd. I wonder what inspired the old bird to do that….

He was pleasantly surprised, though, on entering his new room to discover it was significantly bigger, with a large ensuite bathroom and a balcony which looked out over the horse pastures to the east. The dog basket was on the floor in a corner and, spotting it, the little dog happily trotted over and curled up inside.

Jerry sniffed the air. It was musty and stuffy – obviously this room hadn't been used for quite some time. And then he noticed a small form on the bed.

Another cat! Is there no room in this damned house that isn't infested with these beasts? he thought, as he marched over to the bed to remove the sleeping animal.

Approaching the little creature, though, he suddenly stopped. It was the small black & white cat he had seen in the conservatory. *Poor fellow, there's probably nowhere else in the house where he can find a place to lay his head in peace.* And Jerry decided to leave him be, and turned back to examine the room.

There were some objects that had been left on the bureau that weren't from his valise, and Jerry moved closer to see what they were. There was a small withered cactus, a closed daily agenda, and two pictures in lucite frames, one of the Queen and one of a man in a white lab coat holding a small black & white cat.

Jerry looked at the photograph, then over at the cat sleeping on the bed. Then back at the photograph. It was the same cat.

This must be the good Dr. Chudleigh's room! What luck!

Immediately he set to searching the room, tapping on walls, moving furniture, pulling down framed paintings.

He had pretty-much exhausted all avenues of examination when a soft knock sounded at the door. He opened it a crack and was met with the butler's face.

"I have come to ensure that all is well with your accommodations, Sir," said the butler, who had been alerted by the strange sounds coming from Jerry's room, and who now stood peering over Jerry's shoulder at the displaced furniture and the paintings on the floor leaning up against the wall.

"Yep," replied Jerry. "Just perfect."

The butler looked dubiously at Jerry.

"Was there a problem with the furniture, Sir?"

"Nope! Just making myself at home. Thanks again!" And he gently closed the door on the concerned face.

Jerry walked over to the bed, sat and put his feet up, and reclined against the headboard. Absentmindedly, he stroked the back of the sleeping cat's neck; in response, the cat moved over a few inches and curled up against Jerry's leg and softly purred.

He was sitting there, turning over in his mind various ideas and thoughts, and his eyes settled on the two photographs in their clear plastic frames.

As he contemplated the two pictures the words from a poem he had heard in childhood came running through his mind:

> *Yesterday, upon the stair,*
> *I met a man who wasn't there.*
> *He wasn't there again today —*
> *Oh, how I wish he'd go away!*

And something in his brain went *click!*

He pulled out his phone, called up a shopping website, and tapped out an order.

And then he closed his eyes and, like the little cat at his side, went to sleep.

CHAPTER XI

THE GINGER CAT with the white dot on his forehead couldn't believe his luck.

He gamboled merrily through the garden, pouncing on unsuspecting weeds and rolling delightedly in a warm patch of soil. Life was Good.

After having been confined to the manor for several weeks, the opportunity to once again prowl the wilderness like his ancestors on the African veldt set his primal juices coursing in his veins.

He bounded along hillocks and raced through tiny irrigation channels and finally surmounted a small mound of freshly-turned earth and froze.

There before him, sunning itself on a wide flat rock, was a small baby serpent.

Stealthily creeping up to the unsuspecting snake, the cat hunched down in full Combat Mode, sniffing the air that fortuitously blew toward him from the sleeping reptile.

Tensing his muscles, the cat imperceptibly wiggled his rear and extended his tail straight out behind him, then in a ferocious leap pounced down onto the unsuspecting slumbering serpent and threw it straight up into the air, catching it on its descent in his mighty tiger jaws.

The snake, for its part, was stupefied to have its afternoon reveries interrupted in such a brutal fashion, and was slow to react. Eventually, however, it concluded that this unwelcome attention being lavished on its person by this savage visitor needed to be discouraged immediately, with extreme prejudice.

At which point, just as the cat was about to embark on another exciting round of toss and retrieve, the snake spun its head around and sank its two fangs deep into the cat's front paw.

The cat tumbled back in shock, evidently not having anticipated a hostile response of this nature. The snake speedily slithered off into the grass while the cat staggered backwards, lifting its stinging paw in the air while the paw noticeably swelled in size before its eyes.

Within a moment or two, the cat felt dizzy and determined that a quick rest was in order to clear its senses. It lay down in the grass, and closed its eyes.

AS LUCK WOULD have it, Jerry was relaxing in a front room just off the atrium at precisely the moment when Kat chose to make her arrival.

He was just settling into an armchair with a cup of coffee and the firm intention to do whatever he could to win his way back into Lady Chudleigh's good graces when he heard Trevor – the butler, not the dog – open the front door and inquire, "Yes, how may I help you?"

"Allo allo, Guvnah," came Kat's unmistakable voice, "Oi'm yer new scullery moid, oi yam."

Jerry all but broke an ankle leaping up out of his seat and racing out of the room and over to the door. He skidded to a stop behind the befuddled-looking butler, who had stepped out onto the portico to stand staring uncomprehendingly at Kat.

"Excuse me, miss," responded the perplexed servant. "Might you repeat what you just said?"

Jerry, immediately behind and slightly to the right of the butler, waved his hands frantically around in the air, making whatever gestures he could think of to physically represent to Kat that she needed to speak normally.

He made little "zipping" motions across his lips with his fingers, violently shook his hands side to side and all but jumped up on down in place. He exaggeratedly mouthed the words "NO ACCENT" as clearly as he could, but Kat's eyes betrayed not the slightest glimmer of comprehension.

The butler, his attention momentarily diverted as the back of his neck was gently caressed by the slight susurrations of air generated by Jerry's frantically waving hands and arms, turned and laid eyes on the latter, whose presence he had not previously detected.

Jerry froze in mid-semaphore, looked sheepishly at the butler, and said by way of explanation, "Wow. These flies are really thick out here today, aren't they?"

The butler's steely eyes didn't so much as flicker, but held Jerry in a steady gaze. There wasn't a fly in sight. Flies were actually nonexistent on this planet.

"Indeed, sir," he replied, without so much as a trace of irony.

Kat had apparently twigged to Jerry's intent and wrested back the butler's attention by clearing her throat and continuing, "Ah, sorry, little bit of humour there, mister. I'm trying to say that I'm your new kitchen apprentice, here reporting for duty."

If the butler's previous demeanour had been cool, this last comment rendered it absolutely frigid.

He deployed his trademarked steely gaze on Kat and said forcefully, "*Servants* do not come to the front door." He stressed the word "servants" with a venomous pronunciation reminiscent of the hissing of a pit of serpents.

This left Kat quite nonplussed.

"Well, then," she replied, sincerely puzzled, "How am I supposed to let anyone know I'm here?"

"There is a *rear* entrance," replied the butler. "At the very far back of the house," he added, anxious not to leave any aspect in doubt.

"You present yourself at that location and ring the bell," he continued, sensing that the procedure needed to be spelled out in painstaking detail. "It is clearly marked."

"And who lets me in at that door?" she asked.

"I do."

"Well, it's lucky I've come to this entrance, then, isn't it? I've saved you the trip."

The butler visibly stiffened, not unlike someone witnessing a door being slammed on a person's hand. Jerry wanted to bury his face in his hands, but instead found himself rooted motionless to the spot, mouth agog.

Wordlessly, the butler turned sharply on his heel, and without further comment strode back into the house and firmly shut the door.

Jerry was left on the front portico, staring at Kat, who grinned sheepishly at Jerry.

"Well, I'm not sure I made a good impression there."

"You think?"

"I guess I'll try the back entrance, then."

"The good news is, at least now he knows to expect you."

"Har de har," replied Kat, and then descended the wide front steps and turned to her left, heading off on her journey to the back of the huge house.

JERRY TURNED BACK to the entrance and tried to open the door, but of course it had locked shut behind the butler's retreating form. He contemplated ringing the bell but immediately thought better of it, and instead walked round to the side opposite from where Kat had disappeared. He knew the wide stone walkway that wrapped around the front and west side of the house led to the library and a series of rooms through which he intended to regain entry.

He almost collided with Colin, coming in the other direction.

"Jerry! Just the man I'm looking for! How's it going with the old gal? Are you in solid yet?"

"Ah, getting there…. Let's sit down for a moment."

The two men walked over to a small bench on the edge of the gardens and settled in. Colin pulled a small flask from his suit jacket and offered it to Jerry, who gladly accepted and took a long swig. It had been a hard morning.

"Colin, why did you have me bring that blasted dog here? Do you have any idea what kind of wrench it's thrown into my carefully woven plans?"

Colin looked a bit sheepish and grinned. "Well, Jerry, I couldn't very well have bunged it on her myself, could I? I needed a man of tact like you to break the ice with her. I'm sure she's warming to the little beast already."

Jerry looked at him suspiciously. "You can't be serious."

"Now Jerry, don't take it all so negatively – she's probably quite enamoured with you. You just have to keep it up. The ol' Jerry charm, what? Can't fail."

Jerry rolled his eyes and took another drink from the flask. The two men sat there, passing the flask back and forth and watching the birds in the trees until Jerry rose and said, "Well, I admire your optimism, Colin. I'm glad it's not my neck on the line, though. See you at dinner."

And he headed back up to the patio walkway.

THE FIRST DOORS off the patio that Jerry came to were the French doors for the library, but when he tugged on them he belatedly remembered that they were locked. *Who locks patio doors on a country estate?* he wondered in annoyance.

Imagine his frustration when the second set of doors he came to farther down the walkway were also locked, as were the next.

He was almost about to wave the white flag and yield to calling the butler when he came to the fourth set of doors. Doors through which he could see Lady Chudleigh's darkened office.

The doors which he had opened to allow the ginger cat to exit.

And which he had not relocked after closing.

He pulled gently on the handle. The door opened smoothly.

Silently, he slipped into the office and made his way over to the desk and computer. He extracted a small metal disk from his pocket and clipped it to one corner of the display.

He tapped the screen and was met with the password login box.

Immediately, he called up Kat.

CHAPTER XV

THE BUTLER SEEMED to take an especially long time in responding to Kat's arrival at the rear entrance. *You'd think for such a large fellow he'd move a bit faster,* she thought.

Eventually, however, the door swung open and the butler filled the doorway, peering down at Kat from the stoop.

"Yes?" he inquired, with perhaps a bit more relish than necessary, thought Kat.

"Oh for God's sake! We just had this conversation – I'm here for the kitchen job."

"Quite so, miss. If you would please follow me...."

"I had not been apprised that Lady Chudleigh had taken on more staff," said the butler as he led Kat through the back corridors.

"Keeping things from you now, are they?" said Kat. "That's never a good sign. You know, it might be a good idea to bring your resumé up to date. I mean, just sayin'...."

They passed through a series of hallways until they came to a large, airy kitchen boasting multiple counters, ovens, tall refrigerator-freezers, sinks, and the like. A dizzying array of pots and pans hung from overhead racks throughout the room.

A very round middle-aged woman working at one end looked up at their arrival and smiled warmly at her visitors as she came to greet them, wiping off her hands on a small towel hanging from the apron tie around her waist.

"What have we here, then?" she asked pleasantly, looking at Kat with obvious curiosity.

"Your new apprentice, Helen," replied the butler. "It seems Lady Chudleigh has concluded that your life will be improved with the addition of an aide. I have just confirmed this fact with her in the last moment."

This did not arrive as welcome news for the cook, who had found a singular delight not only in being the Master of Her Domain, but also in the blessed solitude of working in the kitchen far from the distraction of her noisy fellow servants. She visibly grimaced.

"Good Lord, who gave her that idea?"

"I cannot say. Perhaps she has chosen to do her part for society by taking a waif off the streets and teaching it a useful trade."

Kat thought this last little jab was excessive, and she moved the butler's classification in her mental list from the "undecided" column to the "antagonist" category.

The cook, obviously familiar with the pointlessness of arguing with her mistress once the latter's mind was made up, rolled her eyes and said, "Well, can't be helped now. Might as well make the best of it."

Not exactly the warmest of welcomes, thought Kat.

"I shall leave you to it, then," said the butler, turning to leave.

"Hey, hold it," called Kat, before he could make his escape.

He paused in his departure and turned back round to face her once again.

"Yesssss?" was all he said.

"Since you've got a perfectly good door right here" – Kat indicated the kitchen door that opened out onto the back area, close to a small storage building and, further along, the stables – "Why did you make me go to a door on almost the opposite end of this side of the house instead of over here?"

The butler raised his eyebrows fractionally and Kat might almost have detected a small twinkle in them as he said, "Why, so I could open the door for you, of course."

"**WELL, MY DEAR,**" said Helen the cook, regaining her normally sunny disposition and eyeing Kat a little more closely, "Why don't you tell me what your specialty is and we'll see about getting you working."

"Um, specialty?"

"Yes – you know, are you a saucier or a rôtisseur, or maybe even an entremétier – I could actually really use one of those – or do you normally work in the garde manger? Or are you perhaps a pâtissier or a boulanger – do you work in the bakery?"

Kat stood there absolutely dumbfounded while the cook casually rattled off the series of foreign terms. To Kat, she might just as well have been enumerating a list of French fashion designers. However, the cook had ended her inquiry with a word in English that Kat actually understood and – best of all – could also pronounce.

"A baker! Yep. Baker," she said happily. "I work in the bakery."

The cook greeted this revelation with somewhat less than an enthusiastic response.

She sighed heavily.

"Well, I don't really need a baker, but perhaps you can still be of some service. Take off that backpack and go wash your hands and put on one of those aprons hanging by the door."

"What shall we start with, dear?" asked the cook, once Kat was suitably attired. "Do you have any favourite creations?"

"Um, creations…." Kat's mind raced through a list of possible choices that even she could passably attempt. "How about… biscuits?"

"Biscuits." The cook's response was utterly flat and devoid of emotion.

"Mm-hmm," nodded Kat.

Sighing heavily once again, the cook said, "Fine. Afternoon tea is coming up soon, anyway, and we're short on scones. You can make some scones for tea."

The way the cook pronounced it, it sounded to Kat like "skonnz". As she led Kat over to a long metal counter and assembled some mixing bowls and other implements for her to use, Kat silently called up on her Slimlines a recipe for "Skonnz". She hoped it wouldn't be too complicated.

Luckily for Kat the Slimlines were smarter than she was and immediately presented her with a series of recipes. *Ohhhh*, she thought, *scones!*, pronouncing it in her mind like "stones".

Kat selected what looked like the simplest of the procedures, and looked at the cook and smiled broadly.

"Well, I'll leave you to it," said the cook a bit dubiously, and returned to her work stuffing a series of chicken breasts with wedges of ham and cheese.

As Kat worked, she tried to look confident and efficient while both scanning the recipe instructions and preparing the ingredients.

It was precisely at that moment that Jerry chose to phone her. She tapped her teeth together and her Slimlines picked up the call.

"Jerry!" subvocalized Kat as emphatically as she could. "Jerry, this isn't a good time. Things aren't going well right now."

"I can't help it babe. I might not get another chance at this machine. I need your help ASAP."

Kat kept her head down and peered up discreetly through her eyelashes. The chef was still looking down at her hands as she continued her work with the chicken.

"OK then. Just keep it simple and tell me exactly what you need me to do."

"I found the computer and attached the remote, now I just need you to hack the password and find the blueprints file."

Kat busied her hands with random movements while she listened to Jerry's instructions, trying to appear focused on the batter she was preparing.

"OK, give me a minute," subvocalized Kat. A few seconds later she said, "Right, I'm in, let's see…."

Jerry stood back and watched as the screen quickly scrolled through various directories and file lists as Kat's Slimlines efficiently scanned folder after folder.

The cook was discreetly eyeing her from across the room, watching as Kat worked seemingly randomly, picking up first one implement then another, then moving a bowl, then moving it back, and the cook began to suspect that this girl might be mentally deficient in some way.

Just as Kat was about to measure out a portion of flour, the cook called out, "Stop!"

"Not that flour, my dear," she said, as she gently pulled away a box from Kat's hand. "That's for making bread. We should use pastry flour for the scones."

Kat looked around the kitchen, as though she expected to see a large sign hanging from a wall somewhere displaying the words "PASTRY FLOUR HERE".

The cook sighed again. She was really getting in her deep breathing exercises today.

"Go into the pantry and get the pastry flour."

"The pantry…" said Kat, her eyes strangely unfocused and moving randomly back and forth behind her glasses.

The cook rolled her eyes. "Go through that doorway."

"And you want… pastry flour…."

The cook looked like she was about to do violence, either to Kat or to herself. Keeping her voice level, she said, "Yes. *Pastry* flour. In the blue box."

"Pastry flour… in a blue box… pastry flour… in a blue box…" mumbled Kat, as she walked slowly toward the pantry, as though she were trying to keep one set of thoughts in her head as she performed a completely different, particularly demanding task.

The cook watched Kat head slowly toward the pantry, gently bumping into a countertop on her way before correcting her path. *There's something very wrong with that girl,* thought the cook. *I hope she's not on the drugs….*

Kat stumbled out the doorway and turned into the pantry, her eyes frantically flickering away behind her glasses as she searched the file lists scrolling past.

"I'm not seeing it, Jerry – it must be in a hidden subfolder or on a different drive," she whispered. "Let me change the search parameters…."

Peripherally she noticed the shelves in the pantry and briefly paused to glance at the objects carefully arrayed before her. Surprisingly, along the back was a series of hunting rifles, standing vertically, each clipped to the wall. Below them was a shelf holding several boxes of ammunition.

Huh, she thought, *Well now I know where to come if we're attacked by an angry mob….*

She looked to her sides and on a lower shelf to her right she spotted the blue box. As she picked it up she suddenly found a folder marked "house specs" in the list scrolling past her eyes.

She froze the display. "Jerry! I have it. It's in a subdirectory marked 'CLD' – oh, I see, that's the architect they used to build this place, some company called 'Country Living Designs', from what I see here."

"Are you having a problem?" came a voice calling out to her from the kitchen.

"Um, no, I'm good," she called back, and quickly returned to the kitchen with the box in her hand.

The cook was busy at the oven, taking out a sheet of perfectly golden croissants as Kat passed behind her and went directly to her station where she proceeded to pour out a cup of flour from the box and to mix it into the batter.

While she was doing this, using a combination of eye and discreet jaw movements she selected the entire subdirectory and saved a copy on her drive.

Her heartbeat was just starting to return to normal when suddenly the cook, who had come over to check on her, shrieked in horror.

"*Aiee!* What in the name of all that's holy do you think you're doing, girl?" she howled. "This isn't pastry flour, you stupid fool! It's rat poison!"

"Rat poison?" said Kat. "Oh my God, I didn't notice!"

"'Didn't notice'? *'Didn't notice*?" gibbered the cook, fast becoming apoplectic. "Exactly what about this box did you not notice?

"Was it perhaps the big bold words at the top that say 'RAT POISON'?

"Or was it maybe the big red skull and crossbones symbol beneath that? Or maybe," continued the distraught woman, little bits of spittle flecking her lips, "It was the drawing of a dead rat, laying on its back with all four feet in the air and little x's for eyes?"

"Or perhaps it was the little picture on the side of the box," she paused to wave the carton inches away from Kat's face, "Of a tombstone, with the words 'DEAD RAT' written on it?"

"Or how about this –" the woman wasn't done yet – "Where it says on the back of the box in huge letters, 'DON'T EAT THIS, YOU WILL DIE'."

All good points, conceded Kat silently, then grabbed the box from the other woman and said, "But why does it have a little heart at the bottom and the words 'We Love Animals'?"

"Because this isn't normal rat poison, you homicidal idiot – it's a special humane blend that sends the little creatures into euphoric, drugged-out bliss before they peacefully fall asleep and slip over to the Great Beyond."

"Oh," said Kat quietly. "Oops." And she gave a little giggle.

The cook just stared at her, goggle-eyed, for about five full seconds before snapping back into consciousness.

Scooping up Kat's bowl of death, she proceeded to dump its contents into the garbage can before tossing the bowl into the sink and dousing it with hot water.

"We're not even supposed to pour it down the drain, it's so deadly, but I'm at the end of my rope today. I don't have the strength to deal with this. If you'd actually cooked up those scones you would have killed the entire household in one blow."

"You know," said Kat thoughtfully, "Have you ever considered that maybe it's not a good idea to keep a deadly poison in the pantry, along with all the food and stuff?"

"It isn't in the pantry, you fool – it's in the weapons locker, along with all the other death-dealing supplies in this house. The pantry is on the left side of the passageway; the weapons locker is on the right. One would have hoped you could tell the difference."

"Oh. I guess that would explain the rifles…. I thought that was a bit strange."

The cook looked at her with what can only be described as abject pity.

She sighed and said, "You know, we're good here for today. I can handle the rest of dinner by myself. You've had a long trip. Why don't you go up to your room and get some rest? Maybe you'll be more on your game tomorrow morning."

"Oh, that would be wonderful," said Kat, and quickly pulling off her apron and hanging it on the hook by the back door, she grabbed her backpack, spun around on her heel and was out of the kitchen and down the hallway.

KAT TROTTED THROUGH the sprawling manor, passing a seemingly endless array of drawing rooms, dens, libraries, trophy rooms, and every other manner of living space, until she spotted the unmistakable silhouette of the butler at the far end of a hallway.

"Oh, mister butler, sir –" she began, and he looked over at her approaching form and said, "Trevor."

"Where?" said Kat, looking down at the floor and around behind her, trying to spot the little dog.

Adopting the household's latest hot trend, the butler sighed heavily and said, with more than just a touch of exasperation, "No, miss. *I* am Trevor. You may address me thus."

"*Your* name is Trevor, too?" Kat asked incredulously, and then began to laugh heartily. "Oh, that's rich!"

"I have not previously thought it so, miss, but let us not dwell on the matter. How may I be of assistance to you now?"

"My room," said Kat. "I need a room. Can you show me to one, do you think?"

"Indeed," replied the butler. "Follow me."

I should have packed a lunch for this trek, thought Kat as she followed the butler through countless passageways until they finally arrived at a small, windowless room buried in the interior of the upstairs level of the house, near the back.

Kat surveyed the cubbyhole with evident distaste, wrinkling her nose skeptically at the sight.

"What, not even a window?" she asked plaintively.

"Rooms with windows are reserved for the guests of the household, not its servants," replied the butler icily.

"Well, beggars can't be choosers," said Kat, squeezing into the room and tossing her backpack down onto the tiny bed. "Might as well make the best of it."

"Indeed," replied the butler, and immediately disappeared back down the corridor.

KAT CALLED UP Jerry on her glasses and reported that she was a free woman now, and about to start her house reconnaissance.

"Good to hear it, Kat. There's one room in particular that I think you should check out," and he described the strange cold door with the rush of wind passing through.

"Sounds like it might lead to an underground chamber, Jer," she replied thoughtfully. "That would explain the draft and the cold."

"The wine cellar?" offered Jerry helpfully.

"No…. I see that's just off the kitchen," said Kat, scanning the blueprints on her glasses. "I see the room you're referring to, but there doesn't appear to be anything special about it. Maybe it was somehow altered after the house was built. Very suspicious. I wonder if they put in a tunnel."

"We won't know until you get in there. Do you think you can do it?"

"Oh, that won't be a problem, babe. I can pick locks with the best of them. As soon as the house is asleep I'll come down. I can creep around at night pretty well – with my Slimlines I don't need any lights. Makes me the perfect burglar."

"Well, I'm also working on some ideas of my own. We'll crack this thing yet, hon. I'll see you in the morning. Happy hunting."

"You too, Jer," and she clicked off.

CHAPTER XIX

JERRY HAD SLEPT through lunch and now he was regretting it.

Notwithstanding his gnawing hunger, he'd also given afternoon tea a pass, as he hadn't had the courage to slip his knees under the same table as Lady Chudleigh just then, not while the morning's events still burned fresh in his psyche.

And so it was he sat on the balcony of his room in the waning rays of sunlight, gazing out at the horse pastures and tapping his foot impatiently while he waited for the dinner bell.

He noticed that he wasn't the only one in the room who seemed restless. Trevor (dog) was pacing about the room in a decidedly unhappy manner, and kept coming up to Jerry and whining.

Not being a pet owner, Jerry hadn't learned to recognise the signs of a domestic animal with a full bladder. While wondering what in the world was troubling the little beast he himself felt Nature's Call, and the penny immediately dropped.

"Oh, you poor little guy – I know what's on your mind! Give me a sec, we'll get you outside."

After quickly visiting the bathroom, Jerry swept up the little dog and trotted down the stairs and out the library's French doors to the west patio and gardens.

He recalled that the gardener had said the snakes were all tucked away in their hidey-holes in the evening, so he happily released the dog and watched it bound off into the garden.

Settling down onto a garden bench, he pushed out his feet in front of him and leaned his head back to watch the clouds drifting by in the evening sky.

He heard the little dog snuffling around in the garden, and then the sound of paws trotting up to him, followed by a slight pressure on his shoe.

Jerry looked down and saw something in the dimming light that he couldn't quite make out.

"Eh, what's this you've brought me, Tre –" And then the unmistakable visage of the ginger cat with the white dot on its forehead crystallized in his squinting gaze.

The cat was dead. Of that there was no question. It was the deadest cat Jerry had ever seen.

Horrified, he shot bolt upright and frantically whipped his head around to the left and the right, praying that no one was there to witness his intimate proximity with the recently-expired feline.

Seeing no other persons present he breathed a sigh of relief, then quickly scooped up the dead cat and prepared to heave it deep into the bushes at the far end of the garden.

It was precisely at that moment that the butler stepped onto the patio through the library's open French doors and solemnly intoned, "Dinner will be served in fif –"

The butler's announcement was abruptly truncated as he discerned what Jerry was holding in his hand, clearly about to hurl through the air.

Sensing the uselessness of any attempts at discretion, Jerry sighed and walked up to the butler, holding out the dead cat.

The dumbfounded butler automatically extended his own hand and accepted the furry corpse from Jerry, who looked at him somberly and said, "You know, you really shouldn't let the animals out at this time of year. Give this poor guy a Christian burial, won't you?" and proceeded into the house and toward the stairway to his room, the little dog trotting along at his heels.

CHAPTER XX

D**INNER, AS JERRY** had expected, was a decidedly grim
affair.

He got the distinct impression that the wait staff had
been instructed to keep a watchful eye on him lest he purloin the
silverware or attempt to eviscerate the dinner guests with an oyster
fork.

At one point he absentmindedly used his salad fork to scratch
his ankle where the barbarous feline had skewered him earlier and
he noticed the staff standing against the wall all visibly stiffen,
relaxing only when he eventually returned the implement to the
table, at which several of them exchanged knowing glances as if
to congratulate themselves on having thwarted his plans.

They probably believed that if they were to turn their backs
for even a moment every piece of cutlery on the table would
disappear into his pockets and the remaining diners would be
reduced to eating with their hands.

Jerry was familiar with the tale of Police Inspector Javert's
dogged persecution of Jean Valjean, and evidently Lady
Chudleigh was, too. But while Jerry viewed it merely as an
entertaining morality tale, it was manifestly clear that Lady
Chudleigh had embraced it as a training manual, and here the
student aimed to surpass the teacher.

Indeed, Javert's surveillance could be considered nothing more
than friendly child's play in comparison with the penetrating,
beady-eyed stares Lady Chudleigh leveled at her cat-hurling
houseguest throughout the meal. The safety of the silverware was
obviously paramount in everyone's minds tonight.

When the conclave finally came to an end Jerry was up the stairs to his room before the other guests had made it out of their chairs. He sank down on the bed beside the little black & white cat who was once again curled up there.

A relaxing weekend in the country this definitely was not.

*   *   *

Within a few moments of arriving in his room, Jerry opened his door to a soft knock.

The butler stood there holding a small brown package.

"Drone delivery for you, Sir. It arrived during dinner. I did not want to disturb you while you were eating."

Probably afraid it was a bomb to wipe out the whole group in one blow, thought Jerry.

Thanking him, Jerry accepted the package and closed the door.

He unwrapped it and nodded in satisfaction, then set to activating the machine.

KAT CRACKED OPEN the door to her room and peered down the hallway in both directions.

Deserted. The rest of the staff had long since retired for the night and the house was still and dark.

Setting off through the pitch-black hallway she walked as briskly as she could without making a sound. Her Slimlines provided perfect clarity of vision – for Kat, it was as though she were walking down a well-lit passageway in the middle of the day.

The service stairway led straight down to the kitchen and Kat emerged in the little passageway that led to the pantry. She shuddered like a witch coming across a signpost pointing to Salem, and quickly headed off in the opposite direction.

In her haste while attempting to be silent all the doors she passed through she deliberately left slightly ajar; the click of a latch can sound absolutely thunderous in a sleeping house.

Kat hustled through the main hallway toward the front of the house and stopped at the room Jerry had mentioned. She felt the cold breeze swishing past her as she pulled out her lock picks and worked on the door handle.

With an imperceptible *click!* the lock snapped open and Kat opened the door.

She stood there looking at the inside of the room for a moment, then gently backed up and closed and relocked the door. She turned back toward the rear of the house and moved away down the hallway.

AUGUSTUS THE PERSIAN cat knew he wasn't allowed in the kitchen but the temptation of an open door was too great to resist. Besides, he was a cat: the rules don't apply.

Gingerly sniffing around the panoply of delightful smells emanating from all corners of the room, he was inexorably drawn to one particularly succulent aroma wafting down from the large garbage can in the middle of the room.

Leaping up onto its rim, he spied a delicious pool of cake batter sitting puddled in some half melon rinds. Carefully perching on the edge, he lowered his head and began to lap up the delectable batter.

KAT FELT ESPECIALLY groggy the next morning when her Slimlines sounded her wake-up alarm.

She had been up late traipsing through the house, traversing every corridor and scanning every cubbyhole.

And found nothing.

Grumpily, she pulled herself up out of bed in the pitch-black darkness of her windowless room.

9 am! I'm surprised it's even legal to be up this early, she thought. Pulling on her clothes, she made a halfhearted attempt at straightening out her hair, then stumbled out her door and down to the kitchen.

"Good morning," she announced groggily to the cook who was already up working.

"Good morning?! Where have you been? It's almost afternoon!" came the cook's exasperated reply.

"What are you talking about," yawned Kat. "It's only just after 9."

"I thought you said you worked in a bakery! What kind of baker starts work at 9am? Where were you at 4?"

"I'm sorry," said Kat. "Did you say '4'?"

"Of course I said '4'! How else are we supposed to have breakfast on the table at 8 when it takes at least three hours to prepare the dough and bake the morning's pastries? What have you been baking that lets you start work halfway through the day?"

"Um… pizza dough?" answered Kat hopefully.

The cook looked at her with a perfect fish eye. She was clearly in no mood to be messed with.

"Well, now that you're here all the work has already been done, of course.

"I've got to go to the Market to buy the day's supplies. Do you think you can manage to clean up this place and put it into halfway decent shape while I'm gone?"

Kat surveyed the disaster spread out before her. The morning's food preparation had not been restrained, in her opinion. There were more dirty pots, pans and dishes scattered around the room than she had even realised the house possessed.

"Um, sure. I can do that…" she said hesitantly.

"Good," said the cook, untying her apron and heading for the back door. "I'll be back in an hour. I expect to find the place spic and span when I return."

WHEN JERRY AWOKE, the world looked like a beautiful place. Birds were singing outside his window. The sun shone down on verdant pastures flecked with morning dew, and horses frolicked in the fields while gentle breezes tossed their manes around.

The little black & white cat still slept on his bed, but Trevor (dog) was nowhere to be seen.

And then Jerry heard a quiet scratching at his bedroom door.

Opening the door, he looked down and watched in horror as the little dog trotted into his room and dropped at his feet a grey form that lay there motionless.

He recognised it as the old lady's Persian cat, Augustus.

"NO! WHY?! WHY?!" he howled at the dog.

"Why are you doing this? Do you *want* me drawn and quartered? Why do you keep bringing me dead cats?"

The little dog looked up at him and wagged his tail.

Jerry buried his face in his hands and moaned.

CHAPTER XXV

AS SOON AS the cook was gone Kat got to work, but not at cleaning.

During her previous night's explorations she had noticed an impenetrable area directly behind the tall freezer unit that her Slimlines couldn't scan. She hadn't dared to pull the unit out from the wall at that time for fear of making noise that would wake the house, but the cook's serendipitous departure meant she could undertake that exercise right now.

She grasped the sides of the unit and heaved back as forcefully as she could. She was rewarded with a slight squeak as the unit shifted toward her. Encouraged, she kept working the unit back and forth, twisting it out from the wall.

She was making great progress until suddenly she felt something holding the unit back. Peering behind it, she noticed a heavy power cable which was now stretched tight from its wall connection. Grunting, she reached down and with a mighty tug released the cord, then proceeded to pull the unit farther out until she could access the space behind it.

The area which had presented itself to her last night as a featureless blank expanse turned out to be just that – a heavy heat sink mounted to the wall. It was firmly bolted in place and Kat realised it was in no way a candidate for a hiding spot.

She was rubbing feeling back into her bruised hands when Jerry called her up.

"Kat, you need to come up to my room right now," he hissed. "ASAP!"

WHEN KAT ARRIVED at Jerry's door she opened it only to see him standing in the middle of the room holding a very dead Persian cat.

The cat had the strangest expression on its face, almost beatific in nature, with its front paws pressed together as though it were happily clasping an ethereal hymnbook while it sang in the Heavenly Choir.

"Jerry, what have you done!"

"Nothing, Kat! It's this damned dog –" Trevor sat meekly to the side, looking for all the world like butter wouldn't melt in his mouth. "He keeps bringing me dead cats."

"Mm-hm," said Kat skeptically.

"Look, I can't be found with another dead cat, they'll hang me as a witch if this gets connected to me. You've got to take it, Kat!"

"Oh, no you don't, Jerry. You're not palming off your catricides on me. This is *your* mess. Deal with it – I'm busy frying bigger fish of my own."

Kat turned and swiftly departed, leaving Jerry still holding the stiff feline.

He thought a moment, then walked over to the balcony and stepped out, assessing the scene. He carefully measured the vista spread out before him. He hefted the cat in his hand, testing its weight.

He felt very strongly, given favourable air currents and the passable aerodynamics of the cat's corpse, that he could make the pasture from here.

He set his feet in place, took a deep breath, and extending his arm behind him, readied his pitch.

Unfortunately, he failed to anticipate how this posture would look to the little dog behind him, who mistakenly thought Jerry was playing a delightful fetch game.

Just as Jerry put his arm in motion, the dog leaped up and yanked on the cat's tail before falling back down to the floor. This caused Jerry to almost tumble backwards, but regrettably his throwing motion had passed the point of no return.

Losing his balance, Jerry failed to achieve a forward motion with the cat and instead hurled it almost perfectly straight up in the air.

Almost.

Unfortunately there was still just enough lateral trajectory left in his launch that the cat sailed high up and then descended in a narrow arc, just barely missing the balcony railing and disappearing below the edge of the parapet, quickly followed by the sound of a heavy *thwack!*

Horrified, Jerry could barely bring himself to look over the edge of his balcony. When he did, he was greeted with the sight of a very badly crumpled cat laying in a rapidly spreading pool of blood on the patio directly below his window.

"Well, that tears it," said Jerry quietly.

Turning back to his room, he quickly gathered up his belongings, then slung his bags over his shoulder and proceeded to step out onto the balcony and climb down to the ground by shinnying down the drainpipe beside his window.

He was up the driveway and out the gate within five minutes and didn't stop to catch his breath until he was several hundred meters down the road running past the estate.

WHEN KAT LEFT Jerry's room she ran straight down the main staircase and turned into the hallway leading to the conservatory. She realised it was the one place she hadn't searched the previous evening as the room was not on the blueprints, having been added after the house was completed.

Ducking through the doorway, she stopped and assessed the situation.

She set her glasses to IR-LIDAR mode and started scanning the potted plants for hidden spaces or anomalous readings. It was slow work, though, and it took her more time than she had anticipated to work her way through all the greenery.

While Kat was busy scanning the plants, the cook arrived back from Market with her day's purchases. Shopping had gone pleasantly well and she had located all the items on her list in quick measure.

Knowing Kat was working inside the kitchen, she hefted two large paper bags of groceries in her arms and clutched them to her chest as she staggered over to the kitchen door and kicked it several times with her foot. She peered through the glass but couldn't make out Kat inside.

Cursing, she fumbled with her fingers at the door handle, and finally was able to turn it enough to release the latch. She pushed the door open then stomped into the kitchen.

Shuffling her way inside, she was dumbfounded to note that not only was the kitchen in the exact same state of disarray that she had left it in an hour ago, but that the huge freezer unit had been pulled away from the wall near the entrance and now stood almost blocking her path.

Gingerly squeezing her way past the freezer unit, she barely had time to gasp as her foot slipped out from under her as she stepped into a huge pool of water leaking from the unplugged freezer.

As her foot shot out into the air she tumbled backwards and, falling onto her back still clutching the two huge bags of groceries, smacked her head on the kitchen floor and mercifully passed into unconsciousness.

CHAPTER XXVIII

K AT WAS STILL searching the conservatory when she first heard the commotion.

She stopped what she was doing and trotted over to the door, cracking it open.

"– On the patio directly underneath his balcony! And when he tires of murdering cats, who do you think he's going to turn to next?"

The old lady's hysterical voice was piercing in its anguish.

"Trevor, I want you to locate him immediately. Start a room-by-room search. And be sure everyone stays in pairs. We'll be safer if we're not alone."

"I feel I should also mention, madam, that I took the precaution of inspecting the weapons locker this morning and we are missing a large box of Rat Poison," announced the butler in ominous tones.

"Oh my GOD!" shrieked the old lady.

Things are looking grim for Jerry, thought Kat.

Oh well, he can take care of himself. I'd better be getting back to that kitchen.

Hustling back to the kitchen, Kat stopped cold at the scene that met her eyes.

Surrounded by a chaos of scattered vegetables, meats, cheeses, salamis and assorted clusters of fruits lay the cook in a wide pool of water spreading out from the unplugged freezer.

"Oh my stars and little planets," murmured Kat.

She rapidly ran over to the woman and lowered her face down to hers. She thought she still detected breathing. Placing her fingers on the cook's neck she noted a strong, steady pulse. She sighed in relief.

Well, she knew what she had to do now.

Dashing up to her room she grabbed her backpack and stuffed back in the few garments she had brought, then ran back down to the kitchen, gathered some supplies, stepped over the cook's recumbent form and opened the back door.

Pausing at the threshold, she looked back and thought that she really couldn't just leave the poor woman lying there like that.

Grabbing an apron from the hook, she folded it up until it resembled a little pillow, which she gently placed underneath the unconscious woman's head.

"There," said Kat. "That's better."

And she turned and dashed out the door and, leaping over the horse pasture fence, legged it out of there through the pasture toward the trees.

CHAPTER XXIX

AFTER WALKING ABOUT twenty minutes Jerry came to a crossroads beside a gigantic tree.

As good a place as any, he thought. He pulled out his phone and ordered a transport. Pinging his location, the service reported back his expected pickup time.

As Jerry settled down against the tree his phone rang.

"Jerry!" came Colin's hushed voice. "Jerry, are you still on the property?"

"No, I left about twenty minutes ago. Why?"

"I was worried for your safety. The butler's searching the house room by room looking for you. He's carrying his cricket bat, Jerry. And I don't think he wants to invite you to a match."

"Well, don't worry. I have a transport coming to whisk me to safety. By time he determines that I'm in absentia I'll be halfway back to Noom."

"Oh, that's great news, old fellow. And I want to thank you for coming through for me. I'm once again in Aunt Althea's good graces. She's yanked asunder the old purse strings – I'm back in the black!"

"What? How?"

"It's all thanks to you, old bean! She was so distraught at the thought of my working shoulder to shoulder with you she's forbidden me from going back to work! In fact, she's forbidden me from working for anyone else, either – I think she believes my judgment of character might be a little suspect.

"But whatever her reasons I don't care. My heart, as the poet says, *'with pleasure fills, and dances with the daffodils'*."

"Oh you bastard," said Jerry, as the ugly truth suddenly dawned on him. "You planned this all along! You never had any expectation of my charming the old bird – you *wanted* her to hate me. That's why you saddled me with that damned dog!"

"Oh, which reminds me Jerry, thanks for that, too. I told my aunt I needed to rescue the poor little fellow from you before he came to a tragic end and she agreed heartily. He and I are both in like Flynn, my boy."

"Well, I've got to hand it to you, Colin. It was a marvellous plan. Next time you're in my neighbourhood drop by and I'll buy you a drink."

"Mighty sporting of you, old chap. I'd return the offer, but I don't think it would be wise for you to be seen here again. At least not in the next decade."

Jerry hung up and grimaced. Maybe his charm wasn't all he chalked it up to be.

Oh well, Mission Accomplished, even if it wasn't the way he had intended.

CHAPTER XXX

FROM HIS SPOT under the tree Jerry saw Kat when she was still a good distance off, and watched with a grin on his face as her tired form slowly approached. She looked quite bedraggled; thorns and small twigs clung to her clothing, and what appeared to be a string of ivy hung tangled in her hair.

"Out for a stroll?" inquired Jerry as she flopped down in a heap beside him.

"Why do you suppose it is, my dear," she said as she grabbed at the large bottle of water he proffered, "That I always catch up to you heading for the exits?"

"Because I, for one, know when I've overstayed my welcome. I don't need a house to fall on me.

"– And judging from *your* arrival I'm assuming a culinary career is not in the cards?"

"I hate to burst your bubble."

"Well, I can't say I'm surprised, exactly. I've had your lasagna…."

Kat showed him her finger.

Jerry checked his watch then said, "The transport I called won't get here for another twenty minutes. I wish I'd had the chance to bring snacks. I'm famished."

Without a word, Kat reached into her backpack and extracted a long salami.

Jerry's delighted smile only broadened when she followed that up with a baguette and a large thick white disk.

"Bread and salami and Camembert! Tell me you've got some red wine in there too and I'll put you in my will."

"Sadly, no. I had no access to the wine cellar."

"Oh! Speaking of which, what did you find in that room I mentioned? I'm dying of curiosity. Did it lead to a tunnel or a secret cave?"

She looked at him sideways with a measure of disgust.

"Litter boxes, Jerry. Countless litter boxes. Which I suppose makes sense, considering the number of cats in that house."

"So the cold air…."

"Was extra ventilation drawing the odour up and out a special roof vent. Thank God for that, too – even with the enhanced air exchange it smelled quite ripe in there. I'm glad I'm not the maid assigned to clean that room."

Leaning back against the tree, she sighed heavily, a habit recently picked up from her erstwhile employer.

"I suppose I was wrong about that 'Destiny' thing, Jer. I drew a total blank on that house. What a waste of time."

"Oh, I wouldn't go that far, Kitty-Kat," said Jerry cheerily, pausing briefly from peeling a tranche of Camembert with his pocketknife. "Take a look at this." And he showed her his phone.

"Jerry…" Kat began slowly, "Jerry, why is there a deposit from NovoHealth in our account?"

"It's a down payment, honey. It's to show they received the decrypted file I sent them."

"Jerrrrreeeeeeeeeeeee…" Kat squealed. "You did it? But how – when – how did you –"

"Actually, hon, it wasn't hard at all once I gave it some real thought.

"The problem lies in the actual nature of a password storage device, which sort of defeats the purpose, don't you think? I mean, if anyone finds the device, your password is worthless."

"So you just have to hide it well," replied Kat.

"And you know that's well-nigh impossible these days, right? Electronic scanners can be picked up at any garden-variety hardware store. Five minutes with a scanner will find anything buried in stone, cement, underneath water, in your body – you name it.

"So what were we looking for? That's what I tried to figure out. It has to be something so normal it won't draw attention to itself, it has to be portable and always accessible, and finally it can't be anything electronic, for reasons we just mentioned.

"Oh – and it has to contain a string of three billion unique characters not found anywhere else."

"I'm dying here, Jerry."

"Have another bite of salami. The scales are girding their loins in preparation for their imminent flight from your eyes."

Kat sighed. She knew there was no rushing Jerry at moments like this. You just had to cling to the crash bar and hang on until he got to the finish line.

"I figured it all out yesterday, when I was in my room looking at a picture of a ghost."

"A ghost," said Kat.

"Yeah, the words from a poem I'd heard long ago just popped into my head, and I realised suddenly that Percy Budleigh himself was the key to this puzzle. And I suddenly knew how he'd come up with a password with three billion characters.

"That's what gave it away for me – the three billion characters. You know what contains three billion unique characters, Kat?"

Without waiting for a reply he said, "*You* do.

"And I do. We all do. It's called 'deoxyribonucleic acid'."

Jerry was met with a blank stare. Not wanting to miss out on the latest fad, he sighed heavily.

"*DNA*, Kat. The good doctor simply sequenced his DNA and translated it into the public key. And he used the same method to create the private key.

"After I figured that out, I had a handheld DNA sequencer delivered to me last night and I tested my theory. The sample file decoded perfectly and I sent the results to NovoHealth."

"But whose DNA did he use for the private key?" asked Kat.

Putting her hand up to her mouth, Kat said in horror, "Not *Lady Chudleigh's?*"

"No, Kat. Think carefully. It had to be readily accessible to him. He couldn't keep coming here every time he needed to use the password."

"But then who –"

"Oh, and did I remember to mention," Jerry paused to lift the lid of the dog basket Colin had given him, "That I got us a pet?"

As he rubbed his fingers through the fur on the back of the sleeping black & white cat's neck, the animal looked up at him, said "mroww," and laid its head back down, softly purring.

Did you enjoy this book?

If you did, then I'm delighted!

And if you'd like to see more like it, there's one simple little thing you can do for me that's worth its weight in gold (metaphorically-speaking):

Please leave a review!

Your online review will do more for me than you can imagine, and ultimately it will enable me to continue writing more books.

Plus, because I read every review, your review will help me to understand what you liked about my book, so that I can create others that you might enjoy even more!

THANK YOU, in advance.

--J.M. Holmes

About the illustrator

Francesco LaCerva was born more than half a century ago in Palermo on the beautiful island of Sicily, where he lives to this day.

A childhood immersed in films, cartoons, books and comics inspired him to bring to life drawing – first on the walls of his house, and eventually on sheets of paper – the fantastic characters and worlds of fantasy and science fiction.

Today Francesco supports his family, including three children, by working as an established architect. But between his daily commitments designing houses and other buildings, he still feeds his soul with a regular diet of books, comics, cartoons, and film. And ever faithful to his First Love, he dedicates his free time to illustration, never forgetting the passion that has always inspired him: drawing.

See more of his work at https://www.artstation.com/lacerva_art or https://www.deviantart.com/francescolacerva or find him on Instagram: @francesco_lacerva

Francesco La Cerva nasce più di mezzo secolo fa a Palermo, nella bellissima isola della Sicilia, dove vive ancora oggi.

Un'allegra infanzia passata tra film, cartoni animati, libri e fumetti, lo hanno ispirato a riportare in vita disegnando, prima sui muri di casa sua e infine su fogli di carta, i fantastici personaggi e mondi immaginari di fantasy e fantascienza.

Oggi Francesco sostiene la sua famiglia, compresi tre figli, lavorando come un affermato architetto. Ma tra i suoi impegni quotidiani nella progettazione di case e altri edifici, nutre ancora la sua anima con una regolare dieta di libri, fumetti, cartoni animati e film. Sempre fedele al suo Primo Amore, dedica il suo tempo libero all'illustrazione, senza mai dimenticare la passione che da sempre lo ispira: il disegno.

Per vedere altri suoi lavori visita: https://www.artstation.com/lacerva_art o https://www.deviantart.com/francescolacerva o visita su instagram: @francesco_lacerva

About the author

J. M. Holmes was born and raised in Canada and educated in the Classics by Jesuits and nuns who would likely be disappointed to see the results of their efforts.

A Renaissance polymath, Holmes has been the Editor of the bilingual magazine for Glendon College in Toronto; the Editor of that city's French-language newspaper, *Le Metropolitain*; a successful magazine publisher; and Director of the Davis Film Festival in Davis, California.

Recipient of the 2005 *Heroes Award* from the American Red Cross, Holmes has also received commendations from the U.S. Senate, the U.S. House of Representatives, the California Legislature, and the City of Davis, California, in recognition of extraordinary charity work.

Holmes is also the winner of awards in California for running a business with outstanding environmental practices and from Rotary International for producing that charity's weekly publication.

Sadly, Holmes bears some measure of responsibility for the overpopulation of Planet Earth, having participated in the creation of two additional humans, Alex & Sarah, both of whom are college students working hard at honing their skills in questioning authority and challenging conventional wisdom.

Currently, J. M. Holmes resides in the United States and shares a home with seven feral cats. This is one of them:

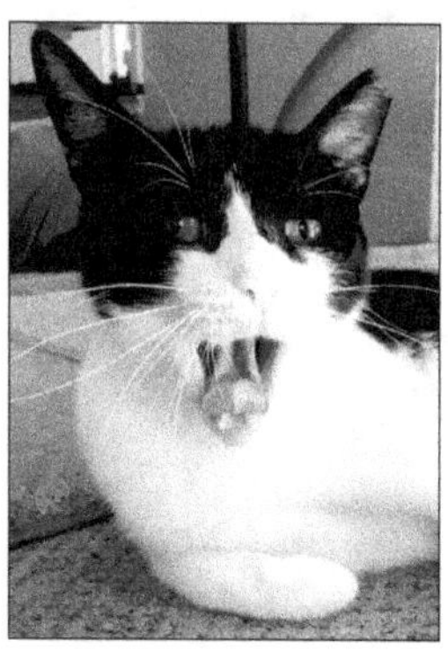

Vedana could hear the keypad beeping quietly as someone entered the door access code sequence. A metallic *click!*, a pause, a hiss, and she heard a footstep inside the room.

She would have bet money that her breathing could be heard throughout the whole ship, it seemed so loud to her. She opened her mouth wide and tried to calm her racing heartbeat, which was humming along at around 200 beats per minute.

She heard the footsteps moving quietly about the room, but they weren't wandering around aimlessly. Whoever they belonged to knew where to go and what to do. There was a quiet efficiency at work here. She heard a few little clinks, a quiet hum of some unknown machine, and the ripple of a zipper being opened and then, a second later, closed.

And then… silence.

Vedana froze. Had she done something to give herself away or left some tiny sign of her presence here?

The intruder seemed to be standing stock still in the dark lab. Listening? Examining the room? What was he doing? Vedana wanted to scream, the tension was so extreme.

And then she heard a quiet footstep come closer to her.

Then another.

The footsteps stopped directly in front of Vedana's cabinet.

She gritted her teeth, and waited for the inevitable yanking open of the cabinet door.

In the mood for something different?
Pick up this new noir crime mystery today!

AVAILABLE NOW!

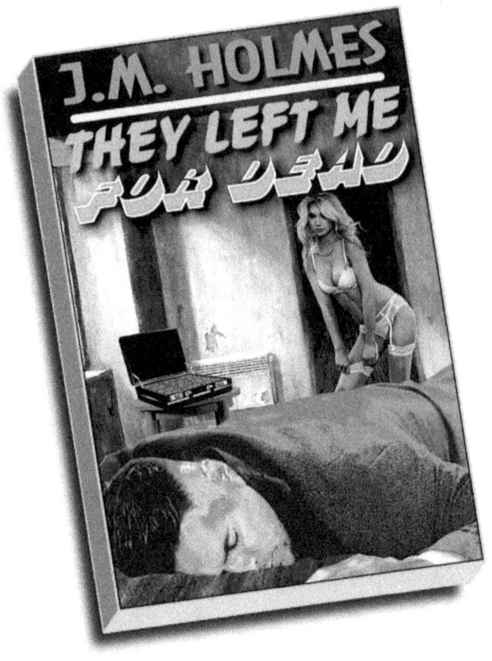

Set in the arid West Texas scrublands, **They Left Me for Dead** dives into dark, dangerous places populated by killers and crooks.

Whether fighting to avoid the hordes of Assassin Bugs that have colonized the region, or working to stay one step ahead of drug-dealers, Mafia hitmen and Mexican cartels, our hero is finding life in his sleepy country town isn't quite as peaceful as appearances suggest.

Featuring a new breed of frontier hero, caught in a tangled web of murder, corruption, and betrayal, **They Left Me for Dead** will draw you in and soon have you sweating along with its hero in the hot, dry Texas Chaparral.

THEY LEAVE ME for dead, lying in a drainage ditch beside the road, and I can hear them as they drive away in my car, just a couple of good ol' boys lighting cigarettes and cracking jokes, as though they're coming back from a fishing trip and not from having just beaten someone to death.

I can't tell you how long I lie here, listening to the rain and the wind and the crickets and all the assorted night sounds that creep back to life after the humans have gone. The stentorian gasps of my own ragged breathing keep time with the persistent rustle of some weeds just off to my left, making me wonder if perhaps some hungry wild creature is assessing my potential as a snack. I am slipping into and out of consciousness every few minutes, and in a grey recess of my mind I peripherally hope that I will be insensate when the beast finally decides to start gnawing on whichever part of my body it's going to eat first.

Every so often a vehicle shoots by in the night, announcing itself first with the quiet hiss of its approach, then gradually crescendoing into a deafening rattling roar defining its identity as car, pickup truck, or 18-wheeler. The weeds around my head sway and buck convulsively as the vehicle whizzes past my location, and then in the wake of its passage quickly resume their motionless witness to my suffering.

I have no way to alert the passing drivers to my presence. I can't seem to move my arms and legs, or even turn my head, either because some part of my spine is damaged or merely just because the intense pain from the rest of my body is overwhelming all my other senses. I know that several of my ribs are broken, along with at least two of the fingers on my left hand. My sides throb in excruciating pain, and I assume that I am bleeding internally from several damaged organs. I can't really see at all from either of my eyes, as both are swollen shut and caked in blood. The taste of blood fills my mouth and I can't breathe through my nose.

I lie here, face down in the dirt and muck, and I wait – for death, or the dawn. I have no way of knowing which will arrive first.

LITERATI INTERNATIONAL

~ SINCE 1984 ~

Toronto • New York • London

Literati International is the privately-held parent company of Literati Media, established in 1984 in Toronto, Canada, which comprises Literati Worldwide Publications, Literati Broadcasting Enterprises, Literati International Reporting & Podcast Productions, and Literati Film and Television Post-Production Services.

Literati International has affiliate partnerships and representatives in numerous countries around the globe, including Australia, India, and Brazil.

Check out the full line of Literati-produced books and media at www.literatiinternational.com